He was five steps away . . . four . . . three . . .

Burt's shoulder dipped and suddenly Clint closed the last two steps quickly, surprising the man. Before Burt could react, Clint swung his left in a wicked arc that ended on the man's jaw. Burt's head snapped back, his eyes rolled up, and he flopped over on his back.

Clint walked on, not looking back. His knuckles on his left hand ached. He had used his left hand because the right hand was his gun hand, and before his visit to New York was through, he might end up needing it.

Don't miss any of the lusty, hard-riding action
in the Charter Western series,
THE GUNSMITH

And coming next month:

THE GUNSMITH #49: SHOWDOWN IN RATON

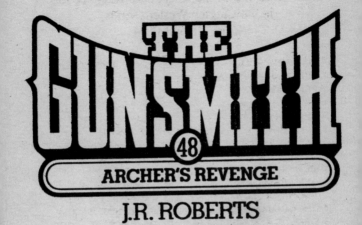

THE GUNSMITH

48
ARCHER'S REVENGE

J.R. ROBERTS

C
CHARTER BOOKS, NEW YORK

The East River Bridge referred to
in this story is better known as
the Brooklyn Bridge.—J.R.R.

THE GUNSMITH #48: ARCHER'S REVENGE

A Charter Book/published by arrangement with
the author

PRINTING HISTORY
Charter edition/January 1986

ISBN: 0-441-30952-6

Charter Books are published by The Berkley Publishing Group,
200 Madison Avenue, New York, New York 10016.
PRINTED IN THE UNITED STATES OF AMERICA

ONE

Clint Adams noticed that he seemed to be looking forward to coming to Labyrinth, Texas, more and more. Directing his rig down that town's main street, he found himself taking in its structures and people fondly—and scolded himself for doing so. The last time he found himself thinking like that people started taking advantage of him, taking him for granted, assuming that because he was a town lawman, he belonged to the town. Clint's declaration of independence came when he turned in his star and began his life as a traveling gunsmith.

He intended to keep his independence, even if it meant coming back to Labyrinth, Texas, a lot less—and maybe not at all.

He took his rig to the livery and turned it, the team, and Duke over to the liveryman.

"I'll take good care of them, Mr. Adams, like I always do," the man promised, and Clint knew enough to take him at his word.

"I know you will, Dan. Thanks."

He didn't have a permanent room at the Labyrinth Hotel—not officially, anyway—but the truth was that they rarely if ever rented the room out, just in case Clint should show up. The hotel's owner, Rick Hartman, had the room saved. He also owned the biggest saloon in town. It was called Rick's Place.

Clint signed the register and took his gear up to the

1

room. His original intention had been to take a bath, but his weariness overtook him as he sat on the bed, and in moments he was on his back, asleep.

The girl in bed with Rick Hartman complained, ''Why don't you put that book down and pay some attention to me!''

Hartman lowered the dime novel he was reading and looked at her. She was a new girl in his place, having come to town the previous month to look for a job. Tall and willowy—the way he liked his women—she had large breasts, slim legs, long, dark hair, and a wide mouth with an underlip that was twice the fullness of its partner. Her bottom lip fascinated him, and he stared at it now as he spoke to her.

''Molly, you're trying to kill me,'' he said, shaking his head. In truth, only a half hour ago had they finished making love for the fourth—or was it the fifth?—time that night.

She bit her luscious lower lip and asked, ''What's so fascinating about that book, anyway?''

She was lying on her stomach, breasts pressed against the sheets, her saucy bottom clearly visible.

''It's about a friend of mine,'' he said, showing her the cover.

''You know him?'' she asked. She pushed herself to a seated position, and he could see her dark nipples.

''I sure do.''

''I thought all those books were made up,'' she said, frowning and taking it from him.

As she began to study the text inside, Hartman looked at the picture and the lettering on the front that said THE LEGEND OF THE GUNSMITH. He said, ''Clint Adams is real and legend.''

"Well," she said, "in that case—"

She tossed the book to the floor, and then moved up on the bed so that she could give her full attention to that part of him that was even now swelling beneath her touch.

"At least this is all for real!"

When Clint woke up, he took that bath he'd wanted. Then he walked down the street to a café he went to sometimes when he was in Labyrinth. After he'd eaten, he'd go to Rick's Place and check in with his friend. He knew there'd be some free meals coming his way from Rick—there always were—but he wanted to pay for the first one.

When Clint entered the saloon, he first noticed the girl. She was tall and slender, so he had no doubt that his friend had staked an early claim, but that didn't mean he couldn't look. She was wearing a lavender gown with a matching ribbon in her dark hair, and when she turned around he noticed her lower lip, which was incredibly lush.

He walked to the bar just as the bartender, T.C., looked up and grinned.

"Clint, by golly," T.C. said. He was a tall skinny man who spoke very little, was good at his job, and had been working for Rick Hartman longer than either of them remembered.

"Hello, T.C., how about a beer?"

"On the way."

"You're him," the woman said, coming up next to Clint and staring at him boldly.

"I beg your pardon?"

"He called you Clint, didn't he?"

"That's right."

"You're Clint Adams."

"Right again."

"Well, I'll be—Rick really does know you, doesn't he?"

"We're good friends. Why?"

She shrugged and bit her bottom lip, which just about made his mouth water.

"I thought maybe he was just talking."

"Not Rick," Clint said, accepting his beer from T.C. "He never talks unless he's got something to say. Is he around?"

"In his office. I'll get him—"

"No need," Clint said, cutting her off. "I'll go on back there myself."

"I don't know—"

"It's all right, Molly," T.C. told her.

"Well, all right, then."

He saw that she was staring at him intently now, studying his face, and he touched the scar on his left cheek, wondering if that was what she was staring at.

"Something wrong?"

"Oh, nothing," she said. "You just don't look the way you do on the cover of the book."

"Book? What book?"

Before she could answer, T.C. said, "Customers, Molly."

Molly looked at the men who were entering the place and said to Clint, "Got to keep the customers happy."

"Well, for someone who looks like you," he replied, "that shouldn't be too hard."

"Ooh," she said, putting her hand on his chest for a fleeting moment, "I think I'm gonna like you."

As she strolled away, Clint looked at T.C. and asked, "Private stock?"

"For nigh on a month, now."

Clint shrugged, and said, "Too bad," and started for Rick's office.

TWO

Clint knocked on Rick's door and then entered. His friend looked up from a book he was reading behind his desk, gaped at Clint, and then abruptly slapped the book down on his desk.

"Clint! Well, I'll be!"

"Hello, Rick," Clint said, approaching the desk to shake his friend's hand.

"Well," Rick said, opening the top drawer of his desk and sliding the book into it in what he hoped was an unobtrusive manner. "Well, well . . ." he said again, inanely.

"You said that," Clint said.

Rick stood up, took Clint's hand, and pumped it enthusiastically.

"How long you in town for this time?"

"Oh, I don't know. I haven't decided."

"Well, it's good to have you here, as always."

Clint sat down in a straightbacked wooden chair. Rick seemed nervous to him and he said so.

"Nervous, me?" Rick said, sitting behind his desk again. "Not me. What have I got to get nervous about?"

"I don't know," Clint said, "but it might have something to do with that book you slid into your top drawer as I came in."

"Book? What book?"

"Come to think of it," Clint said, frowning now, "I met a gal out front who said I didn't look the way I looked on the cover of some book. What did she mean by that, Rick?"

"That must have been Molly. She's something, huh? Did you see that lower lip? Been sinking my teeth into that for about a month, now. Probably time for a change, though. Don't want to get in a rut."

"Lucky you," Clint said. He leaned forward, put his beer mug on the desk, and said, "What book, Rick?"

"Uh, Clint, now listen—"

"I got a better idea. Why don't you just slide that book back out here again and let me take a look at it myself, huh?"

Rick opened his mouth to say something else, but stopped short and complied. He opened the desk drawer, took out the book, handed it over, and waited for the explosion.

Clint took the book and sat back in his chair to examine it. What he saw was a dime novel with a drawing of a man shooting a gun out of another man's hand, and to him neither of them resembled him in the least. However, the block writing at the top of the book fairly shouted out, THE LEGEND OF THE GUNSMITH, so he assumed that one of the men depicted on the cover was supposed to be him.

"Shit!" he said, slapping his knee with the book.

"Is that all?" Hartman said, looking relieved. "Jesus, I thought you were gonna go through the roof."

"No," Clint said, "but the man who wrote this trash is when I get through with him."

"It's not really trash," Hartman said. "It's actually very well written—" He stopped short when he saw that

Clint was staring at him rather coldly, and then he added, "—if a little . . . fanciful with the facts."

"Fanciful?" Clint asked, tossing the book to the desk. "I don't even have to read it and I can tell you that 'fanciful' is putting it lightly. As if I don't have enough trouble trying to live down the name that one damned fool newspaper reporter pinned on me, now some damned fool writer is trying to make it worse!"

"See," Hartman said, "I knew you were gonna go through the roof."

"Who wrote this tripe?" Clint said suddenly, grabbing the book again. "Ned Buntline," he said frowning. "Isn't that the same fella who wrote some stuff about Hickok?"

"He's a very famous writer," Hartman said.

"Where was this published?" Clint asked, and again he answered his own question by opening the book and examining the first page. "New York City."

"You going to New York?"

"You can bet the bank I am," Clint said. "I want to stop this before it spreads too far. One book is bad enough, but more than one—"

"Clint."

"What?"

"There's something I think you should know."

"What's that?" Clint asked, looking up from the book and at his friend.

Hartman reached down, opened the bottom drawer of his desk, and came up with two more books that he placed on top of the desk so that their covers were showing. They each had THE LEGEND OF THE GUNSMITH emblazoned across the top.

"What?" Clint snapped, picking them up. "Three?"

"Three—so far."

"How long have these things been coming out?"

"Every month for the past three months."

"How'd you get them?"

"Saw somebody with a copy of the second one; sent away for the others. I got the rest on order."

"How many are there supposed to be?"

Hartman shrugged. "I guess that depends on how well these sell."

"Well, they aren't going to be selling much longer," Clint said, stacking the three books on the desk. "I'm leaving for New York first thing in the morning."

"Got time for a drink with a friend first?" Rick asked.

Clint picked up his beer, drained it, and said, "You're buying, I assume."

"Don't I always?"

Hartman got up to leave the office with Clint and then, as an afterthought, picked up the books and handed them to the Gunsmith.

"What are these for?"

"Thought maybe you'd like to read them tonight," Hartman said.

"Why would I want to do that?"

Hartman shrugged and said, "Might give you some insight into the man you're looking for."

Clint looked down at the books in his hand and then said, "Good idea! Come on, let's get that drink."

Hartman wondered what Clint would think after he read the books and discovered how well they were written. He might still regard them as tripe as far as subject matter—although *he* was the main subject, and Buntline seemed to know him pretty well. In fact, Rick Hartman was surprised at some of the insight the author seemed to have into Clint's character. These books—though certainly fanciful and loose with the facts—were not quite the outrageous tales that the Hickok books had been.

In fact, they were quite good.

THREE

Clint had more than one drink with Rick before making his way back to his hotel. When he had first ridden into town, he had had no idea that he'd be riding out the very next day—rather, taking the train across the country to New York. He had been born in the east, but had not been there for many years, and had, in fact, never been to New York City.

He was wondering what New York would be like. When he unlocked the door to his hotel room, he stopped short. He saw a woman in his bed. This was not an unusual occurrence for a man of his experience, and it certainly was not unusual for the clerk in the Labyrinth Hotel to let a woman into his room to wait for him. Most of the times he didn't mind at all.

This was one of those times.

"Hello," he said, closing the door behind him.

Sitting fully dressed on his bed was Molly, she of the luscious lower lip, from Rick's Place.

"Hi."

"Been waiting long?"

"Not too long," she said. "Not long enough to get undressed, anyway."

"Well, that shouldn't take very long," he said, removing his gunbelt and hanging it on the back of a chair.

"First, I have to work up the courage," she said shyly, "and I haven't quite done that, yet."

"Courage? For what?"

"Well, after all, you're not really like other men, are you?"

"What do you mean by that?"

"Well, you're . . . the Gunsmith," she said, making it sound as if he were more important than the President of the United States.

"You been reading these books?" he asked, showing her the dime novels. He dropped them on the dresser and scanned the titles briefly: TOWN TAMER, INDIAN FIGHTER, and the third shouted GIANT KILLER.

"Just that last one," she said, her eyes growing wide, "the one about you outdrawing most of the legendary gunfighters in the world, killing most of them." She began to tick them off on her fingers: "Kid Dragon, Dale Leighton, Clay Allison, John Wesley Hardin, Bill Wallmann—"

"That's an impressive list," he said, "considering I've never had occasion to face either Allison or Hardin."

"You were in Abilene when Hardin faced Hickok, weren't you?"

"I was there," Clint said, remembering the confrontation. He had actually cocked his gun in his holster from *behind* Hardin to avoid bloodshed between the kid and Hickok.

"What about you taming Leadtown?"

"I was there—" he said again, but she didn't let him finish.

"Some of those stories must be true."

"Some of them may be true," he admitted, "but there's nothing legendary—"

"I think maybe I should get undressed now," she said abruptly, standing up. "That is, if you want me to."

"Oh, I want you to," he said, nodding, but not if you think it's going to be some kind of a mystical experience between us."

"I don't even believe that."

"Then shuck your clothes, woman."

They each undressed and then regarded each other critically. She was high breasted, with a thin waist and long, shapely legs. A little slimmer than he usually liked his woman, but that full lower lip more than made up for it in this instance.

Apparently she didn't mind what she saw—a slight battered legend, he thought, wryly—and she moved toward him to place her palms against his chest.

He leaned over and chewed on that bottom lip for a few moments, and he found the experience more than pleasant. He pushed his tongue past her lips then, and she, in turn, chewed on him. She snaked one hand between them to grasp his rigid penis, and he slid his hands down over her back to her flanks to cup her tight, smooth buttocks and to draw her closer to him.

They stood that way for a while, groping and feeling, squeezing and tasting, until they moved toward the bed and fell on it together. There they became a little more serious, a little more intense about their tasting and feeling, until they settled into a position where they could use their mouths to gratify each other.

Her crotch was hovering over his face and he reached for her buttocks in order to bring it down to him. He licked her, delving into her from time to time with his tongue, while she held his erection in both hands and slowly slid it in and out of her mouth. Finally, she decided to accommodate as much of it as she could and began to bob her head up and down with increasing rapidity. Since she seemed intent, he fastened his lips on to her and began to lash with his tongue. He could feel her beginning to tremble, and then she was bouncing up and down as her orgasm took hold. He released the hold he'd had over himself and began to spurt his seed.

After that they started their exploration again until she had his organ standing straight and tall, at which time she decided to sit on it, taking it into her and grinding herself down on him. He simply lay beneath her and watched her gratify herself—not that he wasn't receiving any gratification of his own, but she was making all the effort for the moment.

Finally, unable to resist any further, he reached for her and drew her down to where he could reach her breasts with his mouth. He began to kiss and lick the warm, smooth, sweat-covered skin, enjoying the taste of her, suckling her nipples until they were huge, brown nuggets, and then she was bouncing on him again, head thrown back, while he cupped her breasts and squeezed her nipples, intensifying her orgasm with his hands as he emptied into her.

She tried to say something a little later, but he was chewing on her lip again and he didn't catch it. "What was that?"

"I asked you how long you were going to be staying in town?" she repeated.

"Not long, I'm afraid," he said. "I'll be leaving for New York tomorrow."

"New York?" she asked in surprise. "What's in New York?"

"Whoever's been writing those books about me," he

said. Then he corrected himself and said, "That is, about who they think I am. I'm going to New York to show the writer and the publisher the error of their ways."

"Well, we haven't got much time then, have we?"

"No," he said, "we haven't—and we might as well make the most of the time we do have."

After all, he thought, attacking her lower lip again, he could read the damn books on the way to New York.

FOUR

In the summer of 1875 a census of New York City was taken, showing the population to be more than one million—a great increase from the previous census, five years before.

These numbers, had they been known to the Gunsmith, would have staggered his mind.

During the ride, he read the three dime novels that bore his name, and as Rick Hartman had recognized, he, too, saw that they were very well written. Still, he had an argument with the subject matter, although he did admit to feeling flattered to some small degree. He was also surprised to find that some of the incidents were actually factual, though somewhat exaggerated.

He was not flattered quite enough, however, to forgive the author for the liberties he had taken, both with Clint's name, and with the reputation of the Gunsmith.

For that, Ned Buntline was going to be held accountable.

"Ever been to New York before?" the man seated next to him, on the aisle, asked.

Clint looked at the man and identified him as a probable drummer of some sort. He was in his forties, slight, clean shaven and clear eyed, with what appeared to be a drummer's case at his feet.

"No, I never have."

"Lovely city, lovely," the man said, smiling. "Been here many times myself."

"I see."

"Westerner, aren't you?"

Clint looked at the man and didn't have to guess how he had figured that. The closer they'd gotten to New York, the more he began to realize that, dressed as he was—even in the finest clothes he owned—he'd still stick out, especially with the gun on his hip.

"That's right."

"You'd look it, even if you changed your clothes. Planning on getting some new clothes?"

Clint frowned at the man and cautiously asked, "What's it to you?"

"Oh, I'm just making conversation, mister," the man said, "to pass the time. Don't mean no harm. My name's Adam Thatch."

He extended his hand and Clint took it, shook it briefly, and let it go. The man had a small, slender hand, but a surprisingly strong grip.

"If you are planning on some new clothes, I can tell you where to get them. Keep you away from the real expensive stores."

"I'd appreciate that. I'll also be looking for a place to stay."

"I can help you there, too," Thatch said. "The St. Nicholas Hotel is on Broadway between Spring Street and Broome Street. Now, right around the corner, on Broome Street, there's a small shop that sells men's clothes. You can get you a good suit there a lot cheaper than if you went to one of the bigger shops of Fifth Avenue. Mention my name; they know me there."

"How do I get there?"

"The horse-cars will take you there."

"Thanks for the advice and the tips."

"Sure, anytime." He spied the books in Clint's lap and asked, "What are you reading?"

"Just some dime novels."

"They originate from here, you know. I mean, in New York." The man apparently liked to show off his knowledge of New York to strangers.

"So I understand."

"Most of the publishers have their offices down along Park Row and Printing House Square," Thatch continued, still eager to show his knowledge of the big city. "Plenty of antiquarian bookshops down there, too, along Nassau Street."

"Uh-huh," Clint said, beginning to leaf through one of the books as if he intended to continue reading. He did appreciate the man's help, but was starting to tire of his constant talk.

"Well," the man said, "I see you're anxious to get back to your reading, so I'll keep to myself now."

He reached down to his case, opened it, extracted a pad of paper and a pencil and commenced writing. Clint directed his attention to the book called TOWN TAMER, and read again the section about Leadtown, when he had gone there to find out who had killed the town sheriff, his friend Cal Colby. It was one of the more remarkably accurate accounts.

When they finally reached New York, Adam Thatch grinned and said, "Here we are, the big city."

"So I see," Clint said, collecting the bag he had borrowed from Rick Hartman.

"Here, I'd like you to have this," the man said, tearing

a sheet of paper from his pad and handing it over.

Clint took it and was surprised to find an exact likeness of himself drawn on it.

"That's remarkable," he said, staring at it. "It looks just like me."

"Well, thank you, kindly," Thatch said, stowing his pad and pencil back in his bag. "It was a hurried job, but then I like to show off some."

"You've got a right," Clint said. "I thank you for this. Is this your business?"

"Sometimes," the man said, picking up his bag. He hurried into the aisle and told Clint, "I hope your visit to the city is pleasant, friend."

"Thank you."

"See you around," Thatch said and hurried down the aisle to exit.

It was only then that Clint realized two things. First, he had not told the man his own name, and second, with all the talking they had done the man had never once talked about himself. Even at the end there, he had seemed ill at ease about answering questions about his business.

Clint thought about it briefly, shrugged it off, stowed the man's drawing in his own bag, and then moved to join the line of passengers who were getting off.

FIVE

Honest John Kelly—otherwise known as Boss Kelly—was the true successor of the legendary Boss Tweed, who had headed up the Tammany Society during its most powerful and influential—and corrupt—years. Now, Boss Kelly was trying to make people forget Boss Tweed, to the point where it had become an obsession with him.

Kelly, a tall, slender, good-looking man in his early forties, was also serving a term as city comptroller.

Kelly was in his Tammany Hall office on Fourteenth Street, meeting with his henchman, going over his holdings—including the policemen and politicians whom he owned.

When all of that business was taken care of, Kelly closed his ledger books and asked, "What about that reporter?"

Tom Sadler, his right hand man, dismissed the rest of the men in the room, and then turned to face Boss Kelly.

"She's being taken care of."

"When?"

"Soon," Sadler said.

"Who's gonna do it? Some Five Points hoodlum?"

"Didn't you ask me to take care of this, Boss?" Sadler asked impatiently.

Kelly glared and said, "That doesn't mean I'm just gonna forget about it, does it?"

Sadler tried to match his boss's stare, but eventually turned his eyes away and said, "No."

"Who's gonna do it?"

"We're importing somebody from out of town."

"From where?"

"Chicago?"

"Is he good?"

"He's the best."

"Expensive, huh?"

"You said—"

"I know, I said money is no object," Kelly said, holding up a hand to placate his dirty-work man. "All right, Tom, just continue handling it. I've got a meeting today, right?"

"Yes, with Mayor Havemeyer."

"Well, we can't keep hizzoner waiting, can we?" Kelly said, standing up and straightening his vest. He took his jacket from the back of his chair and slipped it on.

"You wearing a gun?" he asked Sadler. The man nodded and patted his chest, where he was wearing a .32 in a shoulder rig.

"Let's go, then."

Sadler started for the door and Kelly put his hand on his arm to stop him.

"When the Chicago man gets here, I want to see him. Got it?"

"Sure, Boss," Sadler said, "sure."

Kelly patted Sadler on the back, grinned his most politically appealing smile, and said, "That's my boy!"

The Chicago killer checked into the Fifth Avenue Hotel

between 23rd and 24th Streets. He bathed, changed into a fresh suit, and then went out to walk in New York. He loved New York City, and everytime he came here, whether on business or pleasure, he first walked to get the feel of it, see if it had changed since the last time. He felt out a city before he went to work in it. It was a ritual with him, and everytime he performed the ritual, the job went all right.

Sometimes he wished he weren't so superstitious, but he was afraid to try it even once without the walk.

He took his sketch pad with him.

Police Officer Tim O'Leary knocked on the door of Captain Fletcher's office and waited to be invited in. When he was—by an inordinately loud, bass voice—he entered and presented himself to his superior.

"Officer O'Leary, sir!"

"I know who you are, damn it!" Ben Fletcher said, looking annoyed and harried, as he always did—and was. Everything annoyed Captain Fletcher. It was the way he lived his life, ever annoyed and never—never!— complacent. Complacency had gotten too many lawmen killed, and he had seen a good many of them go down. Not Ben Fletcher, by God!

"You were assigned to the train station."

"Yes, sir."

"Well, did you see anyone you knew?"

"No, sir—that is, not exactly."

"What do you mean, not exactly," Fletcher said. "We got word that Honest John was importing some talent for a special job. Did you or did you not recognize anyone getting off a train?"

"Well, sir—"

"Speak up, damn it!"

"I saw somebody, sir, who I recognized, but not because I knew him."

"You'll have to explain yourself better than that, O'Leary," Fletcher said wearily.

"Yes, sir. You see, sir, I read these books—er—"

"What books?"

"Uh, the dime novels of Mr. Buntline, sir, and the like—"

"My God," Fletcher said.

"Well, sir," O'Leary went on when it was apparent that the captain as not going to comment further, "I've been reading these new ones about the Gunsmith, sir. Are you—uh—familiar with the Gunsmith?"

"I don't read that trash, O'Leary," Fletcher said, "but any lawman worth his salt has heard of the Gunsmith—though I doubt that man really exists. A figment of some writer's fertile imagination, more than likely."

"Well, sir," O'Leary said, "I did see a man in the station who looked a lot like the Gunsmith—I mean, like the pictures and drawings I've seen."

"And?"

"I followed him, sir."

"And!"

"He checked into the St. Nicholas Hotel, sir, on Broadway—"

"I know where the damned hotel is!"

"Yes, sir. Well, he checked in under the name Clint Adams, sir."

"Adams?" Fletcher asked, frowning. "Isn't that—"

"Yes, sir," O'Leary said, interrupting his superior excitedly, "that's the name of the Gunsmith."

Captain Ben Fletcher's stomach lurched and he belched unhappily.

SIX

The horse-cars were filthy, badly ventilated, and full of vermin. There were traces of straw on the floor of the one Clint was riding, and as winter had just passed, he suspected that they lined the floor with straw when the weather got brutally cold—for all the good it would do.

The driver of this particular car matched the car perfectly. On more than one occasion, Clint saw him being rude to riders, men and women alike, as if they owed it to him to pay their nickel and ride in silence, without complaining.

Clint had asked the man to let him know when he reached his stop—near the St. Nicholas Hotel—and the man had been prepared to reply rudely until he looked into the Gunsmith's eyes. He agreed then and began rumbling to himself, saying beneath his breath all the things he'd been afraid to say to Clint's face.

The St. Nicholas Hotel, at least, appeared to be clean and well kept, and the clerk was polite enough, in a cold, standoffish way.

"I'd like to use your bath, if you have one," Clint said to the man.

The clerk blinked once, stared at Clint as if to see if he was kidding, and then said, "All the rooms have baths, sir."

"Oh, of course," Clint said, feeling like a foolish hick.
"Thank you."

"Of course, sir. Would you like someone to help you
with your bag?"

"No, thanks, I can handle it."

"Someone to show you to your room?"

"I believe I can find it, if it's all the same to you."

"As you wish, sir. Enjoy your stay."

"Thanks."

Clint found his room, reminding himself that he was in
the big city now. There was no need to appear more
foolish than was necessary.

After a long, hot, cleansing bath, Clint decided that the
first thing he would do was get himself a couple of new
suits. He had taken a large chunk of money out of his
account in the Bank of Labyrinth and was determined to
dress himself up proper for New York. At the very least he
expected to get from this trip some high-class, female
companionship—as well as satisfaction from Mr. Ned
Buntline and his publisher.

Prior to going out he rolled up his gunbelt and modified
Colt and buried them at the bottom of his bag, removing
another rig he had removed from his wagon specifically
for this trip. This one was a shoulder rig with a .45 Colt
specially cut down to fit it. It was a single-action revolver,
but he thought he could get by with that while he was in
New York. He had not worn a shoulder rig very often, so
he took the time to adjust it comfortably and make sure
that he could get the gun out as quickly as he wanted to.
Not as fast, perhaps, as with the modified Colt and more
orthodox rig, but quick enough. After all, why would he
have occasion to produce it quickly here in New York?

This was not, after all, the wild, untamed west of Mr. Buntline's dime novels.

Clint found the store the man on the train had recommended, mentioned his name to the man there, and received excellent treatment.

"When will you be needing these suits, sir?" the tailor, whose name was Henry, asked, measuring the length of the trousers.

"I'd like to have them, er, today," Clint said, trying to hide the fact that he'd expected to walk out with them there and then.

"Well, that's a bit tight, sir, but since you're a friend of Mr. Thatch's, I'm sure I can get it done. Are you sure you wouldn't like something a little more, er, colorful, sir?"

Clint had chosen two suits, one black and one a charcoal-gray.

"I'm not all that colorful myself."

"Oh," the man said, eyeing the shoulder rig, "I'm not at all sure of that, sir."

The tailor was a short, stocky man in his late fifties with dusty-gray hair on the sides of a bald pate. He had large muttonchops.

"I'll have the coats cut special, sir, so that the, er, armament will go unnoticed."

"I'd appreciate that."

"Oh, no problem at all, sir. Can you come back in a couple of hours?"

"Is there a café or restaurant nearby where I can get a decent lunch and a good pot of coffee?"

"Of course, sir. You can go into the St. Nicholas Hotel, or there is a place just a little farther down the street called Bogart's. They make a fine apple pie."

"I'll try that place," Clint said. "Thanks again."

"No trouble at all, sir. I'll see you in two hours, then?"

"Yes, thank you," Clint said, reaching for his money.

"No, no, sir," the tailor said. "You can pay me when you pick up the suits."

"Much obliged."

"If I might make a suggestion, sir?" the man said boldly as Clint started for the door.

"What kind of suggestion?"

"Your boots, sir."

Clint looked down at his best pair of boots, which were scuffed and dusty.

"I would advise that you purchase a pair that would be more in keeping with your new clothes, sir."

"And would you know of a place?"

"Yes, sir. Just between here and Bogart's there's a bootery. Just tell the proprietor that Henry sent you over. He'll take good care of you."

"Everyone in New York is taking good care of me."

"It's a friendly city, sir."

"Those are the ones you've got to watch out for," Clint said, and left the man frowning at his last words.

SEVEN

At the café called Bogart's Clint enjoyed a fine meal, served to him by a young, flirtatious waitress who had the sturdy calves of a woman who spent most of her time on her feet. Her name was Ruth McDonald and Clint made a mental note to check back there again should female companionship prove otherwise difficult to find. He liked sturdily built gals.

On the way to the tailor shop he picked up a fine pair of black leather boots to go with his suits. When he returned to the tailor shop, Henry would not let him leave unless he wore one of the suits. They chose the charcoal-gray and Clint left the tailor shop clad in new finery.

Walking back to the hotel, he did not feel quite as awkward as he had when he'd first left the hotel—and he couldn't help but wonder how he looked.

As he entered the lobby, he spotted the clerk at the desk beckoning to him. Could he have a message waiting for him already? And if so, from whom? Rick Hartman? Could something have happened to Duke?

"I feel I should advise you, sir," the clerk said, "that there was a policeman here asking about you."

"Asking about me?" Clint said, surprised.

"Yes, sir."

"I can't imagine why," Clint replied, genuinely puzzled. "He didn't happen to say, did he?"

"No, sir. He merely described you, checked the register to see what your name was, and then left—warning me not to say anything to you about it," the man added pointedly.

Clint recognized that as a ploy for money and gave the man what he hoped was an appropriate amount for New York City.

"Thank you, sir."

"Tell me something," Clint said, "why did you tell me about it?"

"I do not like policemen, sir," the man said, "and I do like money."

"What's your name?"

"Justin, sir."

"Well, Justin, let me know if anyone else shows any interest in me and there'll be more money in it for you."

"I'll be alert, sir," the clerk said, "of that you can be sure."

As Clint ascended the stairs to the second floor, Justin—who was born and raised in the Five Points section of New York and considered his present position a huge step up—tucked the money away in his pocket and nodded across the lobby to a man seated in a chair on the opposite side.

In his room, Clint hung up his other new suit and then tried to decide what he could do that evening that would do his new suit justice. He wasn't much for the theater, and he supposed that he could probably find a poker game somewhere, but he would much rather have found a young—or not so young—lady to while away the evening—and the night—with him until morning, when he'd start looking for Ned Buntline.

He wondered why a lawman would be asking about him already, his first day in New York. Was he that well known that someone had spotted him at the train station, or on the street? Should he have checked in with the local police upon his arrival to avoid that?

He decided that in the morning he'd go to the police, introduce himself, and then ask them to direct him to Ned Buntline's publisher.

Tonight, however, was still to be dealt with—and there was always the waitress at Bogart's.

After making his report to his captain, Tim O'Leary had made the same report to his other boss—Boss Kelly.

"Do you know what he's talking about?" Kelly asked Sadler.

"Some legend from the wild west," Sadler said, shrugging.

"Maybe not just a legend," Kelly replied. "Find out, Sadler."

"Sure, Boss."

It was for that reason that Sadler had been in the lobby of the St. Nicholas when Clint came back with his new clothes. The clerk had been telling the truth, because O'Leary *had* checked the register prior to making his dual reports. What Justin had not told Clint was that he had only called him over to the desk in order to point him out to Sadler, for which he had been paid much more than Clint had paid him.

Justin never forgot Five Points, or how fast Boss Kelly could send him back there.

Clint had dinner in the hotel dining room and then decided to go for a walk. In the back of his mind he felt that he was going to end up at Bogart's, just in time to walk Ruth home after they closed.

It was dark, and the echoes of footsteps on the paved sidewalk—rather than bootheels on a wooden boardwalk—and the *clip-clop* of horses' hooves on the cobblestone street were strange sounds to his ears.

As he turned into Broome Street and began to walk toward the café, he passed the tailor shop, which was closed, and then the bootery—also closed—before he became aware that he was being followed. It took him that long because it was totally unexpected, even after the clerk had told him about the police. Was it the police who were following him?

The answer came as he reached the next street corner. A man stepped out into his path and planted himself there firmly, twenty feet away. At the same time, the footsteps behind him quickened, and another man appeared on the other side of Broome Street and began to cross over.

Clint stopped and unbuttoned his jacket for easy access to his gun. Not police, he decided—possibly robbers.

As he turned, the man behind him stopped, and the man crossing the street did also. The other man still had not moved.

"Something I can do for you boys?"

The man who stood in the street answered.

"Throw your wallet down on the ground and you can keep walking, can't he, Burt?" he asked the man in front of him.

"Right past me," Burt agreed. His tone was amiable, but his stance remained solid. The man who had been following him remained silent.

"I don't think I can do that."

The man in the street shrugged.

"You look new in town, mister—nice new clothes,

new boots. Maybe you don't know the way we do things here. You from the west?''

"That's right?''

"You ain't wearin' a gun,'' the man said. "Don't everybody in the west wear a gun?''

"I guess that's for you to find out.''

"Should I go get a gun so we can settle this in the street, like in Abilene?''

The mention of Abilene made Clint think of his friend, Wild Bill Hickok, who had been killed by a coward's bullet fired from behind. Were these men cowards?

"I'm going to walk past your friend Burt, there,'' Clint said, pointing to Burt. "Anybody who tries to stop me is not going to be doing much walking after tonight.''

Clint began to sidle toward Burt, keeping an eye on all three men as best he could. He didn't think he had to worry about the one who had followed him. He was just there to add to the numbers. The one in the street, the leader, he seemed more ready to talk than to act.

Burt was another story.

Clint decided that this was some kind of a test, although he didn't know why, or for what. If Burt was the test, there was no point in avoiding it.

He turned his back on the other two men and walked toward Burt, a big man with sloping shoulders. A bully, surely, and a strong man, too.

He closed the gap steadily, and Burt betrayed himself by shifting a foot slightly.

He was left-handed.

Clint did not expect a gun, and although a knife was possible, he didn't seriously entertain that thought, either. More than likely Burt would use his fists, which meant that Clint would not be able to use his gun. He was going to have to beat Burt at his own game.

He was five steps away . . . four . . . three . . .

Burt's shoulder dipped and suddenly Clint closed the last two steps quickly, surprising the man. Before Burt could react, Clint swung his left in a wicked arc that ended on the man's jaw. Burt's head snapped back, his eyes rolled up, and he flopped over on his back.

Clint walked on, not looking back. His knuckles on his left hand ached. He had used his left hand because the right hand was his gun hand, and before his visit to New York was through, he might end up needing it.

EIGHT

Ruth McDonald was waiting for him.

"How did you know I'd come?" he asked, stepping into the doorway with her. He could smell the mixed odors of all the dishes she had served during the day, but there was also the pure female smell of her—her musk, her sweat, her sexuality.

"You're a stranger in town," she said, shrugging. "I didn't think you'd be able to do better—at least, not tonight."

"Ruth—"

"Hey, I don't mind," she said, holding up her hand to stop him. "I know what I want, Clint, and I'm willing to give you what you want—for tonight or for however many of your New York nights you want. After that, you'll leave New York and forget me."

"Ruth—"

"Don't argue with me," she said, taking his hand. "Walk me home." He took her arm and led her out of the café.

"Where do you live?" he asked as they got to the street.

"Near Five Points, but don't worry. Nobody will bother you as long as you're with me."

"Five Points?"

"Oh, that's right, you don't know about Five Points. Well, that and the Bowery are probably the roughest—and poorest—neighborhoods here in New York. The poor usually turn to crime to get what they want, so many of our New York hoods come from there.''

''And you?''

''Yes, I come from there—but I'm trying to get out.''

When they reached her apartment on Mulberry Street, he followed her into a building, which looked ready to fall down, and up a flight of stairs that wavered like a drunk.

''Don't say anything about the place,'' she said, pulling him along with her. ''It's a hovel, but it's all I can afford right now.''

When she opened the door to her rooms, he saw that she was nearly right. It had once been a hovel, but she had fixed it up so that now it was a near hovel.

''We could use a lamp,'' he said.

''No,'' she said, ''no lamp. We can use the moonlight for what we want.''

She was right. The moonlight streaming through the window was enough once you were in the room for a few moments and your eyes adjusted to the dimness. He hoped that she didn't want the lamp because the room was a mess and not because she had some sort of scar to hide.

She turned to face him and said, ''I wanted you as soon as you walked into the restaurant.''

''That's very flattering.''

''Come here.''

He moved closer to her until they were almost touching.

''I know I have a plain face,'' she said, ''but I'll show you that I make up for it in other ways.''

''You don't have to make up for anything,'' he said, putting his left hand on her hip. She was as firm as he had assumed when he first saw her. He put his other hand on one of her breasts and found it hard and full.

She unbuttoned the top of her waitress's uniform, took

his hand, and slid it inside. Her nipples nestled against his palm and began to harden. Her skin was smooth.

"You're hard," he said, meaning it as a compliment. He squeezed her breasts to bring this across.

"So are you," she said, after putting her hand on his crotch. She was excited, her voice coming out breathlessly, as she rubbed her hand over his stiffening cock.

She pushed him away then and began to undress and he followed suit. They examined each other in the moonlight, and they were very much alike in that they were both without an ounce of fat. Clint was lean, however, while Ruth was full-bodied. Full-bodied women were often soft, though, with a likelihood of going softer as they got older. Ruth appeared to be in her late twenties, but Clint knew that she would be as hard at forty as she was now, and her breasts would not sag at all. He knew women who would kill for breasts like hers, that stood out almost straight from her chest and would flatten out very little even when she was lying on her back.

He kissed her then and her slim lips were mobile on his, her tongue skillfully alive in his mouth. Already he was sure that he knew what she'd meant when she said she'd make up for her plainness in other ways.

Her hands were roving over his body eagerly, and he slid his hands down her back until they were gliding over the opulent curves of her ass, tight and muscular.

Wanting to make it up to her somehow for thinking her plain—which, of course, she was—he went down on his knees before her, sliding his lips and tongue over her breasts and nipples. He licked her navel, her belly, all the while maintaining his hold on her buttocks.

She leaned on his shoulders as he slid his tongue down through the tangle of hair. She moaned and when he plunged his tongue into her he felt her buttocks clench. He gripped them tighter as they did. Avidly he continued to lick her, working his tongue in and out, thoroughly enjoying the taste of her. He teased her, coming near her core time and again, encircling it until *he* couldn't take it anymore. He closed his lips and began to maneuver his tongue. Her breathing began to come in longer, harder gasps until she sounded as if she were sobbing. She was gripping his shoulders tightly, and then, as she came violently, she began to beat on him with her fists until her legs gave way and she fell on the bed. Going with her, he refused to release his hold on her, either with his hands or his mouth, and she began to writhe on the bed, riding out the tremors that were wracking her firm body until they faded and left her aching for more.

Losing none of his eagerness, Clint worked his way back up her body until he was devoting his attention to her breasts, holding them in his hands, sucking the nipples, marveling at how full and firm they were.

"All right, my darlin'," she said, "it's my turn."

She lifted his head away from her breasts and pushed him over onto his back. She encircled his nipples with her tongue and began to work her way down his body until her face was nestled between his legs, her nose nuzzling the crown of his erection.

"Mmm," she moaned, sliding her tongue over it and then licking her way down the underside until her tongue was laving his balls. She worked her way back up and she opened her mouth and took him in as he lifted his hips, letting her slide her hands beneath him.

In moments her head was bobbing up and down on him, her hands squeezing his buttocks, and he could feel his orgasm welling up inside of him and was afraid that it would be over before it started.

Ruth would not allow that, however. She extricated one hand from beneath him and encircled the base of his penis with her thumb and forefinger. The geyser that was building up inside him subsided, but her mouth was still avidly working the length of him and, when she released the hold of her thumb and forefinger, he again began to feel it.

"Jesus, Ruth . . ." he moaned and he could have sworn he heard her giggle, even with her mouth full.

"Come up here," he said abruptly, reaching for her. He grasped her beneath her arms and pulled her up until she was lying atop him.

"You have an incredible body, Ruth."

"Breeding stock, my grandfather used to say," she said, tracing his lips with her tongue. "All of the Mc-Donald women made good breeding stock."

"Well, I don't know about that," he said, "but if all the McDonald women are like you, they're probably a pleasure to be around."

"Well, you'll never get to find out," she said. "I'm keeping you to myself. Let my sisters, cousins, aunts, and dear old mother find their own men."

She moved her hips up off him, reached between them to take hold of his cock, and then settled down over it, taking it inside slowly, inch by inch, until he was nestled safely and firmly within her.

And a better place to be he could not have imagined.

She began to ride him slowly, easily, just letting him ease in and out of her in long, deep strokes. She sighed each time she took the full length of him inside her, and when she planted her palms against his chest, he sensed that she was about to increase her pace. Leaning her weight on her hands, she began to ride him faster and faster until she was almost bouncing up and down on him.

As solidly built as she was, she was heavier than she appeared to be, and she jarred his hips each time she came down on him. He reached for her and pulled her forward so that he could reach her breasts with his mouth. He began to suck on her furiously and she responded by moaning and crying aloud in response to the dual stimulation of his rigid penis and avid mouth.

He was trying to hold his own orgasm in check, waiting for her, and when he felt her begin to tremble, he knew it was time. He began to spurt inside her just as her orgasm hit, and she crushed her breasts against his face and jammed her crotch down against his, kicking her legs so hard that he was afraid she'd fly off him, and he wrapped his arms around her and held her tightly to avoid that happening.

"Oh, my God!" she shouted and then she screamed.

"Won't someone worry about that scream?" he asked.

It was only minutes later and she was still on top of him, with his cock softening inside her.

"This is Five Points, Clint," she said with her lips against his neck. "Nobody is going to wonder about one little scream."

"Little?"

"I'm sorry," she said, lifting her head so she could look at him, "but it's . . . never felt like that for me before. I've had a lot of men, Clint—though I don't want you thinkin' me a whore—but none has ever done to me what you just did."

"Bring out your brogue, you mean?"

"Damn," she said, frowning, "I hadn't noticed that."

"Why do you try to hide it? I think it adds to your already considerable charms."

"Do you, now?"

"I do."

"Well, then, maybe I'll be lettin' it loose around you even more, but at work it wouldn't do. Not everybody likes the Irish as much as you do, Clint Adams."

"I can't see why not," he said, squeezing her buttocks. "I don't have any complaints."

She kissed him then, a deep, probing kiss that he returned with interest, and as his hands roamed over her again, he knew one thing for sure: There were certainly no scars or blemishes that he could feel—and he'd had his hands and mouth on everything there was to feel.

They made love again, slowly and with obvious enjoyment of each other, and then Clint rolled away from her and said, "I'm paying a lot of money for a hotel room. I'd better get back to the St. Nicholas and use it."

"You can't."

"Why not?"

"This is Five Points, Clint," she said. "You wouldn't be safe walking around alone out there."

"Don't you walk home alone every night?"

"Sure, but I live here. Nobody's going to bother me. You're a stranger."

"Ruth—"

"Of course, I could walk you back, but then I'd have to walk back here alone."

"You just said—"

"I know, but anything could happen, couldn't it?"

"Well, then," he said, "you'll just have to come back to the hotel with me and stay the night. You can go to work from there in the morning."

She shook her head in wonder and said, "Me, in the St. Nicholas?"

"It'll be their pleasure."

They dressed and when they left Ruth took some fresh clothes with her.

"You'll be able to take a bath in the morning," he said.

"Are you trying to tell me something?"

"Well, we're liable to work up a sweat . . ."

"Are you sure you wouldn't rather just leave me here—just in case you should find something better?"

"It would be impossible for me to find someone better," he told her, knowing that it was what she wanted to hear.

It was true, though. He might be able to find someone prettier, but certainly not better.

NINE

As Clint and Ruth entered the lobby, he looked at the desk reflexively and the clerk, Justin, began to beckon to him as he had done last time.

"Here's the key," he said, handing it to her. "Go up and wait for me."

"All right, Clint."

He watched her as she went up the steps and then went to the desk.

"What is it, Justin?"

"You wanted to know, sir, if anyone else showed an interest in you."

"That's right."

The clerk inclined his head and Clint looked in that direction. There was a man sitting on a round divan, well dressed, in his forties, with a tightly clipped mustache. He nodded to Clint, who returned the nod.

"Uh, sir?"

"Yeah?"

Justin said, "The management frowns on guests bringing women into their rooms for the purposes of, uh—"

"That was my cousin, Justin."

"Oh," the clerk said, nodding, "I guess that's all right then, sir."

"Thanks."

Clint left the desk and walked to the man on the divan.

"I understand you're interested in me."

"If your name is Clint Adams, I am," the man replied, looking up at him.

"That's me."

"Well, I could stand up," the man said wearily, "but then we'd both just have to sit down again."

"Why would I *have* to?"

The man smiled and said, "My name is Hoyt, Dick Hoyt." He produced a badge and said, "Lieutenant Hoyt of the New York City Police Department."

"Mind if I sit down?" Clint asked.

Clint sat next to Lieutenant Hoyt, who said, "I just have a few questions, Mr. Adams."

The respectful tone in the man's voice told him he wasn't in trouble—yet. "Go ahead," Clint said.

"What are you doing in New York?"

"I came to look for a man."

"What man?"

"Ned Buntline."

"The writer?"

"That's right."

"What for?"

"He's been writing some books about me," Clint said. "I'm not very happy about it."

"Why not? I've read one or two of them and think they're pretty good."

"As far as they go, they're fine, but I've already got a reputation that I've got to live with, Lieutenant. Those stories could end up making it a little harder to do."

"I know your reputation, Mr. Adams. That's why I'm here. My captain—Ben Fletcher is his name—asked me to come over and check you out."

"Why?"

"A man with a reputation comes into our city, we like to keep an eye on him."

"I was coming to your office in the morning, just to check in."

"Well, that's good to hear," the man said. "I think Captain Fletcher would appreciate that."

After a few moments of silence Clint asked, "Is there something else, Lieutenant?"

"You'll have to forgive me, but I've got only your reputation to go by. We've heard that . . . a killer has been imported from out of town to do a job here in New York."

"And you think I might be that man?"

"That's what the captain told me to come over to find out."

"Would it satisfy you and your captain if I told you that I don't hire my gun out?"

"Your reputation—and those books by Mr. Buntline—would make that hard for some people to believe."

"That's what I'm here to see Mr. Buntline about."

"Well," Hoyt said, standing up, "I appreciate your talking to me, Mr. Adams."

"No trouble, Lieutenant."

"You—uh—might want to stop by the station anyway in the morning, to see the captain."

"A city this size must have more than one police station."

"That's a fact," Hoyt said. "Police Headquarters, however, is on Mulberry Street, between Houston and Bleecker Streets. The superintendent is Mr. George W. Walling, but Captain Fletcher is the superintendent's right hand man, you might say. He's displaced at the moment, being assigned simply to run interference for the superintendent. I can tell you, some of our inspectors resent him greatly, but I think you'll find him a fair man."

"You seem to have a high opinion of him."

"As I said," Hoyt repeated, "he's a fair man."

"All right. I'll stop by to see him first thing."

"And then go looking for Mr. Buntline?"

"Yes. Do you know where he lives?"

"No, but you might try his publisher in Printing House Square."

"I'll do that."

"Good night, Mr. Adams."

"Good night, Lieutenant."

Clint watched the man walk out of the hotel, impressed with the way he had handled the questioning. His instinct told him that Hoyt was a good lawman. He hoped that the same could be said for the man's superior. He didn't need to muck up his stay in New York by running afoul of the local law.

When he knocked on the door to his room, Ruth answered, holding a towel wrapped around her. Her arms and shoulders glistened with water, and her hair was wet. The towel was small, so that he could see all of her long legs also glistening from the bath. The top slopes of her breasts also glistened.

"I decided I couldn't wait until morning to take a bath," she said as he stepped in and closed the door behind him. "What took you so long? Another woman?"

"No," he said, kissing her nose. In the bright light of the wall lamp he noticed the spray of freckles on the bridge of her nose. "I had to see a man about . . . a reputation."

"You mean yours?" He frowned and she said, "I

found these books on the dresser over there. Do you like reading about yourself?"

"No, I don't. That's why I'm here in New York, to see if I can keep any other books from coming out."

She walked to the dresser where the books were, dried her hand on the towel, and picked one up to examine.

"Should I read one? Will I be impressed?"

"You might," he said, moving toward her and taking it from her hand, "but I'd rather you weren't. I'd rather you were impressed by what you see—what I am."

With that he pulled the towel from around her and dropped it to the floor. Instinctively, she sucked in her stomach and thrust out her breasts, but these movements weren't necessary. She had a marvelous body, which he had already discovered by studying it in near darkness. Now he wanted to examine it in the light—and he took his time doing it.

He lifted her in his arms and carried her to the bed. When he dropped her on to it, she stared at the ceiling and said, "I can't believe I'm going to do it in the St. Nicholas, with a man they write books about."

"Forget the books," he said, "but you can count on the other on one condition."

"What's that?"

"Just don't try to hide that brogue when we're together, okay?"

"Sure and it will be so thick you'll be tripping over it, sir," she promised.

"I'll hold you to that."

He undressed and joined her on the bed. She had freckles between her breasts, too, and he began to lick them.

"They don't come off," she whispered, cupping his head in her hands.

"Um," he said and kept licking until he reached her nipples. Her skin was dark, but her nipples were even darker, chocolate brown. He kissed and licked them for some time, and then he abruptly turned her over.

"Clint," she said in surprise.

She moved down so he could examine her ass and said, "You have a wonderful behind."

"Enjoy it," she said, wiggling it at him.

He began to kiss it, nipping it now and then, and then running his tongue between the two firm cheeks. He moved around and she spread her legs so that he was positioned between them, and he spread her cheeks so he could tease her anus with his tongue.

"Now," she said, "please make love to me now, Clint."

He pressed the head of his cock against her and then slowly worked his way inside her. She was incredibly tight.

"Ooh!" she said.

"Feel good?"

"Very," she said, and then added, "You're incredible."

She moved her hands over her breasts while he was still moving on top of her.

"Oh God, yes," she said, then, "I'm going to—I am, I'm—oooh!!"

Her orgasm came and he felt her clench him and suddenly his seed was sucked from him and he was filling her. She had a hand over her mouth to muffle her screams because, after all, this was not Five Points.

TEN

In the morning she watched him dress, staring with interest as he slipped into the shoulder rig and checked the cutdown .45 before depositing it firmly into the holster.

"I'm going to read these books," she said, rolling on to her back with one of them in her hands.

"Don't you have to go to work?"

"Not until noon."

"I wish you wouldn't read those," he said, slipping into his jacket, "but if you do—" He stopped and she looked at him, frowning. "Well, if you do," he continued, "just don't believe half of what you read."

"Will you come to the restaurant for lunch?" she asked as he walked to the door.

"I don't know where I'll be at lunch time," he said, "but I left the key on the dresser. Feel free to come back here after work."

"Sure," she said.

She got off the bed and he watched as she walked toward him, her breasts so full they moved very little. He enjoyed the way the muscles in her legs bunched as she walked. She kissed him, and then he watched her buttocks in fascination as she walked away from him.

"I'm going to take another bath," she announced.

"Help yourself," he said. "I'll see you later, Irish."

Police Headquarters was known as "the Central Office." As Hoyt had said, it was located on Mulberry Street, between Houston and Bleecker, a handsome structure of white marble that also extended through the block to Mott Street, where its front on that street was brick.

The Central Office housed the offices of the commissioners and their clerks, the superintendent, the street cleaning bureau, the detective squad, the chief surgeon, and the rogue's gallery. The building was also connected to each of the city's thirty-five station houses by special telegraphic wires.

Clint presented himself to the sergeant at the front desk and announced that he'd like to see Captain Fletcher.

"You got an appointment?"

"Sort of," Clint said. "I believe he's expecting me."

The policeman looked around, spotted another uniformed policeman, and said, "Patrolman, take this man up to see Captain Fletcher."

"Sure," the other man said. He looked at Clint and said, "Follow me."

Clint followed the man up a flight of steps and down a hall lined with doors. They came to one that seemed to have recently been marked CAPTAIN FLETCHER and the patrolman knocked.

"Captain, someone to see you," the patrolman said after he'd opened the door.

"What's his name?" Clint heard a gruff voice ask.

The patrolman, looking embarrassed at not having asked, turned to look at Clint and asked, "What's your name?"

"Adams, Clint Adams."

The patrolman relayed the name and Fletcher bellowed, "Well, let him in here, damn it!"

"Yessir!" the patrolman said, and stepped aside to allow Clint to enter.

"You have breakfast, Adams?" a beefy man in his fifties asked from behind his desk.

"Uh, no, I haven't. I came right—"

"You want some coffee?"

"Sure, that'd be fine."

"What's your name?" Fletcher asked his patrolman.

"Swan, sir," the man answered. "Harry Sw—"

"Get some coffee, Swan, and make it fast."

"Yessir!" Swan said, and backed out of the room, closing the door.

"Sit down, Adams."

Clint took a seat directly in front of the captain's desk.

"I appreciate your coming over here, Adams," Fletcher said. "Tell me something, are you everything they say you are?"

"Who are they?"

"You know," Fletcher said. "The people who make up the reputations until they grow unwieldy and difficult to live up to. Are you everything they say you are, Mr. Gunsmith?"

Clint thought of several possible answers to that question and then simply said, "No."

Fletcher regarded him for a few silent moments, the silence broken by the arrival of Police Officer Swan and the coffee.

"We'll pour," Fletcher said, taking the pot from the tray. "Get out."

Fletcher poured two cups of coffee and handed one to Clint.

"What are you doing in New York, Mr. Adams?"

Clint, assuming that the captain had heard it from his lieutenant, but wanted to hear it again for himself, told him about Buntline and the novels.

"Oh yes, Mr. Buntline," Fletcher said. "I've heard that he's supposed to be a good writer."

"I'm sure he is," Clint said. "I have no quarrel with that."

"Just with his subject, eh?"

"That's right."

"Well, listen, just how mad are you at Mr. Buntline? I mean, certainly not mad enough to kill him, I hope."

"I thought I'd already answered your question earlier, Captain, about whether or not I'm what *they* say I am?"

"So you did. You're not in town for any other reason than what you've told me, is that right?"

"That's right. I'm staying at the St. Nicholas, I don't know how long I'll be here, and I intend to try to enjoy your city during that time."

"You wouldn't mind if I had a man follow you around, would you?" Fletcher asked. "I mean, it would be for my own peace of mind, as well as yours. I'm sure you'd feel very safe with a lawman behind you."

"I could have used him last night."

Fletcher frowned and asked, "What's that mean?"

Clint told him about the run-in he had with the three men on Broome Street.

"The big one sounds familiar," Fletcher said, "and if it's who I think it is, I'm impressed, Mr. Adams."

"I'm not," Clint said, holding up his left hand to show the captain his swollen knuckles. "They still hurt. Who do you think it was?"

"Well, I'd rather not say, but if you'd care to swear out a formal complaint, I can have it checked out."

"No, thanks."

Clint stood up to leave and said, "Thanks for the coffee, Captain."

"Let me explain something to you before you leave, Adams," Fletcher said.

"Go ahead."

"There are thirty-five precincts in this city, and each of them has a station house almost like this one. In each of those station houses is a captain, and his responsibility is to see that his precinct is run smoothly and with as little crime as possible. Now, I'm a captain, Adams, but I'm special. The superintendent has said that, not me. A lot of people don't like me because of that, and I mean my fellow captains and such on this police force, but that doesn't bother me. Do you know why?"

"Why?"

"Because I've got a job to do, and I don't care who dislikes me because of it. Do you know what that job is?"

"I get the feeling you're going to tell me."

"My job is to keep tabs on men like you, strangers who come to town with reputations in their hip pocket. Trouble follows men like that, don't you agree?"

"I do," Clint said without hesitation.

"Good. Then I think we understand each other, Mr. Adams."

It was *Mister* Adams, again.

"I think so, Captain."

"Fine. Now, what about that man on your tail?" Fletcher asked. "Any objections?"

"Not if he can keep up," Clint said.

"Oh, he'll keep up, Mr. Gunsmith," Fletcher said to himself as Clint left. A stranger in town couldn't hope to elude one his home grown police officers.

Could he?

● ● ●

At Tammany Hall Honest John Kelly's man Sadler was giving him a report on Clint Adams's movements of the night before.

He told him about the three men he'd had face off with the Gunsmith in the street, about the waitress he'd gone home with and then brought back to his hotel, about the man he'd spoken to in the lobby of the hotel, and then finished by telling him that Adams had gone to see Captain Fletcher only that morning.

"Why would he go to see the police?" Kelly wondered aloud. "And Captain Fletcher yet, Superintendent Walling's own man?"

Sadler shrugged. "Maybe just a courtesy call. He is, after all, a former lawman himself."

"Send some telegrams," Kelly said. "I want to find out how much of what they say about this man is true?"

"Why?"

"We may be able to use him."

"For what?"

"I haven't decided that yet," Kelly said, pinning Sadler with a hard stare. "After you check him a little further, I'll decide."

"Sure, Boss," Sadler said, "sure."

"What about the man in the lobby of the hotel?"

Sadler shrugged and said, "Just a man. My man didn't know who he was."

"He could have been a policeman."

"Maybe."

"Find out."

"All right."

"And how is our little plan going?"

"I haven't had any contact with our man—"

"Why not?" Kelly demanded, cutting the other man off.

"That's the way he works," Sadler explained. "I won't see him until after the job is done."

"I don't like that."

"That's the way he works—"

"You said that already!" Kelly snapped. "I still don't like it, but I guess there's nothing I can do about it—this time."

"Yes, sir."

"All right, get out and get those things done. I've got a meeting today."

"Yes, sir."

"And don't 'yes sir' me too often, Tom," Kelly said. "Just get it done."

"Right, Boss."

Kelly watched Sadler leave the room and then got up to go to his meeting on the second floor. It was with a lovely young thing from a Broadway line who had been very flattered that Boss Kelly had wanted to meet her—and had stayed the night.

ELEVEN

Almost all of New York City's leading morning and evening daily newspapers and publishing houses were located in large buildings in and near Printing House Square. This is a triangular place on the east side of the City Hall Park at the north end of Park Row. In the center of the open space is a bronze statue of Benjamin Franklin, which was erected by the printers of New York.

Walking through the square, Clint saw the offices of New York's largest newspapers. There were approximately twelve daily newspapers; seven evening papers; ten semiweekly; two hundred weekly; and about twenty-five magazines. Clint Adams had only a vague knowledge of two of these papers, the *Herald*, which he knew was privately owned by James Gordon Bennett and was located at the corner of Broadway and Ann Streets, and the *Tribune*, which had been founded by the famous Horace Greeley and was located at the corners of Nassau and Spruce Streets.

It was Mr. Bennett that Clint Adams wanted to see because it was a small publishing house that he owned that had published the particular novels that he was interested in. Through Bennett, Clint hoped to locate Ned Buntline.

The building that housed the *Herald* was a magnificent structure of white marble, easily the most conspicuous building in the square. Clint entered the lobby and advised

59

a uniformed guard that he wanted to speak to Mr. Bennett. The guard gave him directions to the editorial offices, which were located right on the first floor.

Once he'd located those offices, he spoke to a middle-aged woman at a desk and told her that he wanted to speak to Mr. James Gordon Bennett.

"I'm afraid Mr. Bennett is out, sir."

"When will he be in?"

"Oh, no, you don't understand, sir," the woman said apologetically. "He is out of the country, in Europe. You can speak to Mr. Savitch, however. He is in charge in Mr. Bennett's absence."

"Fine, I'd like to speak to Mr. Savitch, then."

"Do you have an appointment?"

"No, I don't have an appointment."

"Oh," she said, looking as if that were very bad news, indeed. "What is it in reference to?"

"Some novels that one of Mr. Bennett's publishing houses puts out."

"Oh, well, Mr. Savitch wouldn't handle that, sir."

"Well, who would?"

"Which books are we discussing, sir?"

He grimaced and said, "The Gunsmith books."

"Ah, well, that would be Mr. Bennett's Western Publishing House. Their offices are at the other end of the hall. You can ask for Mr. Holman. He is the editor."

"Thank you," Clint said, wondering how much more of this he was going to have to go through.

He walked down the hall until he came to a door marked EDITOR, WESTERN PUB. HOUSE. He entered without knocking, expecting to have to deal with another woman. Instead, there was a man sitting at a desk in a room that was barely larger than a closet.

"Can I help you?" he asked, looking up from his desk.

He was a slight man with thinning hair and glasses. His fingertips were smudged almost black, and there were some fingermarks on his face.

"You can if your name is Holman."

"That's me, George Holman." He squinted at Clint and asked, "Are you a writer?"

"No, I'm not a writer."

"Good. I can't deal with any writers today."

"Why not?"

"They're all crazy," Holman said. "Egomaniacs. They think the world can't live without the gift God gave them. If you're not a writer, what can I do for you?"

"I'm looking for a writer."

"You an editor for another magazine?"

"No."

"Why do you need a writer? You want your life story written up?"

"I'd like to find Ned Buntline."

"Really? Why do you need Buntline?"

"I'd like to talk to him?"

"About what?"

"The books he's been writing."

"For me? The Gunsmith books?"

"Yes."

"What about them."

"I don't like them."

The man shook his head and said, "What are you, a critic or something?"

"Or something," Clint said. "My name is Clint Adams."

"Adams, huh? Which paper do you—" Holman started to ask when he stopped short, recognizing the name Clint had used.

"Adams?"

"That's right."

"Uh, the Gunsmith?"

"Right again."

The man regarded Clint for a moment with a mixture of awe and disbelief, and finally disbelief won out.

"Get out of here!"

TWELVE

"Wait a minute," the man said after Clint had spoken to him for a few moments. "Are you trying to tell me that you're really the Gunsmith?"

"Didn't you think I existed?"

"Well, to tell you the truth," the man replied, "no. I mean, I figured there was somebody out there named Clint Adams, but that the stories were exaggerated."

"They were."

"Oh—well then, what can I do for you?"

From the look on his face the editor still wasn't quite sure he believed Clint, but that was okay. "Can you tell me how to find Ned Buntline?"

"Well, we really are not in the habit of giving out our writers' addresses."

Clint remained silent and waited.

"Besides," Holman said, beginning to fidget in his chair, "he doesn't write the books."

"What?"

"Buntline doesn't write the books."

"He doesn't? Well, if he doesn't, who does?"

"Well, I can't really tell you that—"

Clint put his hands flat on the man's desk and leaned over so that the editor had to shift back to avoid contact.

"Look, Mr. Holman, I've come a long way to talk to

whoever has been writing those books. Now, either you tell me who it is, or I'll leave here and go to see a lawyer.''

"A lawyer? What for?''

"To see if I can sue this rag for writing unauthorized stories about me.''

"Unauthorized stories—'' Holman said. "You'd never be able to sue Mr. Bennett—''

"So I'll sue you.''

"Me? What for?''

"You edit this rag, don't you? You approve what goes into it?''

"Mr. Bennett's the boss—''

"Look, all I need is a name and address. I just want to talk to whoever's been writing the books.''

"No trouble?''

"Not if I get the name.''

"Look, I could get fired real easy,'' Holman said. "Bennett's gone through a half dozen editors already—''

"He won't hear it from me.''

The man thought it over quickly and said, "All right. It's a woman—''

"A woman?''

"That's why we decided to use a man's name—because a lot of people would have reacted the way you just did.''

"Why Ned Buntline? He's a big name, isn't he? Why would he lend his name to something he didn't write?''

"We rented his name. Besides, he looked at the stuff and said it was pretty good. The only one who didn't like the arrangement was the woman, but we told her that if they were good we'd let her start using her real name . . . eventually.''

"All right,'' Clint said, "what's her name?''

Holman hesitated a moment, then took a deep breath, and said, "Archer, J.T. Archer."

The name took Clint's mind back to Leadtown and a crusading young newspaper editor named J.T. Archer, a beautiful blonde who had wanted very much to do a Gunsmith story in her paper. Clint had never had any intentions of agreeing, no matter how close he and J.T. might become.

And they had become very close.

Eventually, he had agreed to an interview, the results of which he had never seen.

Now, after all these years, it seemed that the young editor had come east and become a full-fledged writer, and the first thing she'd written about was the Gunsmith.

No wonder some of the things in the books rang so true. She had heard them right from him.

"All right," he said to Holman, "give me her address."

Before going to look for J.T., Clint stopped at one of the small restaurants that lined Printing House Square. He got a table in a corner, from where he was able to hear most of the conversations that were going on—most of which had to do with publishing.

He wondered idly whether Ned Buntline was among the diners.

In point of fact, there was really no reason for Clint to talk to Buntline now that he knew who had really written the books. He had allowed Holman the small victory of withholding Buntline's address.

"Sir?" a waiter said, appearing at his elbow.

"Oh, good afternoon."

"Afternoon, sir. What may I get for you?"

Two of the three men at the nearest table were dining on slabs of prime rib that looked perfectly cooked, so that's what he ordered, along with vegetables, rolls, and coffee.

"A full pot."

"Yes, sir."

As an afterthought he said, "Would you be able to bring me a newspaper?"

"Yes, sir. We have some complimentary copies for diners—but you will have to return them before you leave."

"Of course."

When he brought the coffee pot, the waiter also brought copies of the *Herald* and the *Tribune*.

"I'm sorry, but these are yesterdays," the man said. "It seems today's are being read."

"That's all right."

Leafing through the paper, Clint wondered how J.T. would look now that she was a more mature woman. He wondered, too, if her personality had changed much from the crusading seeker of justice she had been in Leadtown.

The answer came to him in the *Herald* when he found an article with the byline, J.T. Archer.

He read it with interest, even after his lunch came, and found that as far as being a seeker of justice she had changed very little. The article was apparently one of a series speaking out against someone named Boss Kelly—otherwise known as Honest John Kelly, and it was J.T.'s contention that he wasn't so honest, after all.

Apparently the man had political ambitions, and Clint wondered how J.T.'s articles would affect those ambitions.

He put the paper aside to concentrate on his lunch. Then he paid and returned the newspapers.

"I hope they were all right, sir," the waiter said.

"They were fine," Clint assured him, tipping him generously, "just fine."

He left the restaurant and headed uptown to see J.T. Archer at her home—on Sutton Place.

When he arrived there, he was surprised—no, shocked. J.T. had done very well for herself, judging from the kind of neighborhood she was living in. It was ten steps above Five Points—maybe even more. There wasn't much more above this.

As he tried to enter the three-story building, he was stopped by a man wearing some kind of uniform.

"Who are you?" he asked.

"The doorman, sir. Are you here to see someone?"

"That's right."

"Who, may I ask?"

"J.T. Archer."

"Oh, Miss Archer," the man said with a funny, un-readable look on his face.

"That's right."

"Would you wait right here, sir?"

"Sure."

The man went inside and disappeared for a few minutes, then reappeared with another man in tow. Judging from his appearance, Clint assumed that the stocky man was a policeman.

He assumed correctly.

"You're here to see Miss Archer?"

"That's right."

"What's your name?"

"Clint Adams—what's yours?"

"My name is Hocus, Mr. Adams," the man said, "Detective Hocus."

''Is there some problem, Detective?''

''Well, were you a friend of Miss Archer's?''

''Some years ago, yes, but—what do you mean, *was* I a friend?''

''I'm afraid Miss Archer is dead.''

''What?'' Clint asked, shocked. ''What happened?''

''She was murdered, Mr. Adams, apparently some time last night.''

After a moment Clint found his voice and said, ''Can I see her?''

The detective hesitated a moment, then said, ''Sure. Follow me.''

Clint followed Hocus up the steps to the top floor where the man led him into a sumptuous apartment. On the floor by an oversize divan was a body, covered now with a blanket. There was another man in the room who, after a look at Hocus, stepped away from the body.

Clint squatted by the body, reached down, and pulled the blanket enough to look at J.T.'s face. She looked serene, as if she were asleep, and she was even more beautiful than he remembered.

He covered her up again. He was about to stand up when he spotted something underneath the divan. He looked at the two policemen, but their attention was occupied by something on a writing desk in the corner. He reached under the divan, picked up a crumpled piece of paper, and put it into the inside pocket of his jacket.

As he stood up, Hocus turned away from the writing desk and asked, ''What did you say your name was again?''

''Clint Adams.''

He had a book in one hand and a sheaf of papers in another. As he held the book up, Clint could see that it was one of the Gunsmith novels.

"This Clint Adams?"

"That's right."

"Mr. Adams," Hocus said, as his partner pushed back his jacket to reveal his gun, "I think you'd better come with us to the station. We'd like to ask you a few questions."

THIRTEEN

On the way to the local police precinct, Clint invoked the name of Captain Fletcher, and that earned him a change of destination. When they got to Mulberry Street, they went straight to Fletcher's office. Clint waited outside with a patrolman watching him, while Detective Hocus and his partner went inside. He recognized the patrolman as Swan, the one who had taken him to Fletcher's office during his previous visit.

No one had bothered to disarm him, or even check to see if he was armed.

After a few minutes the door to the captain's office opened and Hocus stuck his head out.

"Come in here, Adams."

Clint got up and entered the captain's office.

"Adams," Fletcher said, scowling at him, "I thought you told me you were going to keep out of trouble?"

"You've had a man on me, Captain," Clint shot back. "He'll tell you I've done just that."

Fletcher looked embarrassed for a moment and Clint knew that the man who must have been following him had lost him somehow.

"Never mind that," Fletcher said. "Sit down."

"Am I under arrest?"

"No."

"Under suspicion?"

"Of what?"

"Anything."

Fletcher hesitated a moment and then said, "We just want to ask you some questions."

"All right," Clint said, sitting, "ask."

"How well did you know the dead woman?"

"I knew her some years back in Avalon, New Mexico, a town also known as Leadtown."

"What did she do there?"

"She was a journalist, same as here."

"What about these?" Hocus asked, pointing to one of the novels and a stack of writing paper on Fletcher's desk.

"What about them?"

"How do you feel about these novels?"

"I don't like them."

"Did you tell her that?"

"I came here to tell Ned Buntline that."

"Well, apparently she'd been writing them and using Buntline's name," Fletcher said.

"Then maybe you'd better ask Mr. Buntline how he felt about that."

"We intend to," Fletcher said, "but right now we're discussing you."

"What do you want to know?"

"Did you know she was writing them?"

"I just found that out today by visiting the *Herald* building."

When he mentioned the *Herald* building, Fletcher looked uncomfortable.

"Is that where your man lost me?" he asked. "In the *Herald* building?"

Fletcher scowled.

"Don't blame him, Captain," Clint said. "That place is a maze of hallways."

"Never mind that," Fletcher snapped. "Why did you go to Sutton Place today?"

"Like I said, I just found out that J.T. was writing the novels. I went there to talk to her about them and to renew old acquaintances."

"You sure you didn't go to see her last night?" Hocus asked.

"Last night I was in the company of a young lady."

"Where was this?" Hocus asked.

"Five Points, and then my hotel. You can check it out with her."

"I will. What's her name?"

Clint told the detective Ruth's name and where she worked, and then he offered that the detective would probably be able to find her at his hotel later that evening.

"We're having dinner," he added.

"Fine."

There was an awkward silence then and Clint broke it by asking, "Is that all?"

"For now," Fletcher said.

"Then can I ask some questions?"

"Why not?"

"How was she killed?"

Fletcher looked at Hocus, who said, "With a knife. It was clean and professional."

"I read a newspaper for the first time today," Clint said. "It seems she was writing some pretty inflammatory articles about someone named Boss Kelly."

"You stay away from Boss Kelly, Adams, if you know what's good for you," Hocus said. "This isn't the west. He'll chew you up and spit you out."

"Is that a fact?" Clint said, looking at Hocus, but his expression was one of intense annoyance, bordering on anger. Hocus noticed the look and subsided.

"Look here, Adams," Fletcher said, "I hope you don't have any plans to look for the girl's killer yourself. This is police business."

"I'm well aware of that, Captain."

"Well, just remember that if you get in my way I'll throw you in jail."

"Are you going to investigate this personally, Captain?"

"You can go, Adams," Fletcher said without answering Clint's question.

"Should I wait outside for your man?"

"Just get out of here, and don't plan on leaving New York for a while."

"I wouldn't think of it," Clint said. "I've got a funeral to attend."

"Uh—yes," Fletcher said.

Clint started for the door, then stopped and turned to the captain again.

"Captain?"

"Yes?"

"Would you let me know whether or not her publisher or somebody pays for the funeral? If not, I'd like to take care of it myself."

"I'll let you know."

"Thank you."

Clint left the office and made his way to Mulberry Street. He decided to go back to his hotel to think about everything that had happened that day.

Suddenly, those damned novels did not seem so important anymore.

FOURTEEN

In the midst of a crowd on a horse-drawn car Clint Adams began to remember J.T. Archer . . .

J.T. Archer had been a woman of about twenty-five when he first met her. She had long blond hair and blue eyes. She had been about five feet four, slim with well-rounded breasts. She had been wearing an ink-smudged apron over jeans and a work shirt, and she had also had ink beneath her nails.

She had been the prettiest thing he had seen in months.

He had been in Avalon, Texas, to find the killer of his friend, Sheriff Cal Colby. J.T. Archer had been a crusading young newspaper editor, having inherited the paper from her father. She had been eager to help Clint, eager to interview the Gunsmith . . . and eager in other ways, as well.

Her skin was the palest he'd ever seen, even for a blonde. Her nipples were pink; her breasts small, lovely and round. When he had touched her nipples with his tongue, she had drawn her breath in sharply, and after he had sucked them to hard little nubs, she'd exhaled shakily.

She had professed to love him, but he'd been unable to return the emotion. She'd understood.

When he had entered her, she had become a wild thing beneath him. She'd bitten, scratched, clawed, beat her heels on his buttocks and lifted them both off the bed with her hips when her time came.

Coming back to the present, he realized that he'd been sitting there with a vacant expression, remembering how lovely, how eager J.T. had been—about her work and being in bed with him.

And now she was dead.

He didn't bother trying to con himself into believing that he loved her, but he had liked her very, very much. Whoever had killed her shouldn't be allowed to get away with it.

And he had no intention of allowing that to happen.

He thought about Fletcher's taking such an interest in this particular murder case and felt that it had to be because of J.T.'s articles about Boss Kelly.

High on his list of things to do, then, was meeting Honest John Kelly.

When Clint returned to the hotel, he found Ruth waiting for him in his room, fresh from a bath.

"You're going to get all wrinkled," he said as she kissed his cheek. Again, she had one of those short towels around her and was making no attempt to use it to cover much of her. Under normal circumstances she'd have been a stirring sight.

She picked up pretty quickly on the fact that this was not a normal circumstance.

"Something happened?" she asked.

He looked at her and said, "Yes." He removed his jacket, and his shoulder rig.

"What?"

"The police might be here later to question you."

"About what?"

"About where I was last night."

"You were with me last night," she said, and then added, "and any other night you say, Clint."

He put his hands on her wet upper arms and said, "Thanks, Ruth, but just tell the truth. I don't have anything to hide."

"What is it all about?"

"Someone I knew once . . . the woman who wrote those books . . . was killed last night."

Ruth waited a few seconds and then asked, "A woman wrote those books?"

"Yes."

"I've read them, you know."

"And?"

"They were very good—even if I didn't believe half of what was written."

"Good."

"The woman," Ruth said, then. "Was she . . . very beautiful?"

"Very beautiful," he said thoughtlessly—and then realizing what he'd said, turned to her. Suddenly she was trying to use the skimpy towel to cover herself.

"I'd better leave—"

"There's no reason for you to leave."

"Were you in love with her?"

"I hadn't seen her for years, Ruth," he explained. "I didn't even know she was in New York."

"Then . . . you didn't come here to see her?"

"No. I only found out she was here earlier today. I went to see her because I found out that she was writing those books. When I got there, the police were ahead of me . . . and she was dead."

She touched his arm and said, "I'm sorry . . . and I'm sorry I got . . . jealous."

"That's all right."

"When will the police be here?"

"I don't know," he said, "later maybe. Why don't you get dressed and we'll go down to the dining room for dinner."

"All right."

She moved to the bed, where she had some clothes laid out, and dropped her towel. On her smooth, muscular buttocks drops of water glistened, and if she was a stirring sight with the towel, without it she was . . . breathtaking.

He came up behind her as she was reaching for her clothes and slipped his arms around her waist.

"We can eat," he said, sliding his hands up to cup her breasts, "later."

"Well?" Boss Kelly asked Tom Sadler.

"It's done."

"Have you seen your man yet?"

"Tonight—to pay him the rest of his money."

"All right," Kelly said. Then nodding to himself, he repeated, "All right."

"There is one thing, though."

"What?"

"Our man at headquarters, Swan, says that Clint Adams was taken in to see Fletcher."

"Why?"

"Apparently he knew the dead woman a few years ago, and our man says he seems to be ready to take a personal interest in finding her killer."

"Did you check him out?"

"Yes."

"And?"

"If he's not the legend he's painted to be, he's pretty damn close."

"Let's not get carried away, Tom," Kelly said. "Let's just assume that he's a dangerous man."

"All right, what do you want to do about him?"

"Ask your man if he'd be willing to take on another job—if the need should arise."

"It'll cost more."

"Well, of course, it will cost more," Kelly said, annoyed. "Every damn thing costs more these days. Just have him stand by and we'll use him if we need him."

"All right," Sadler said. "I'll tell him."

"Give him a deposit," Kelly said, "and tell him he may get a crack at a legend. That should hold his interest."

FIFTEEN

Dinner passed undisturbed, and Clint assumed that the police would be coming by late, probably in the person of Detective Hocus. Maybe they hoped to catch them in bed, thereby putting them at somewhat of a disadvantage.

"That was the best meal I ever had," Ruth said, as Clint poured her another cup of coffee. "You're spoiling me, Clint. I don't know what I'll do after you're gone."

"You'll get by, Ruth."

"Yes, I probably will," she said. "I'm pretty much a survivor—but then, some people survive in better style than others."

"Find yourself a rich man."

"That's not a bad idea."

They were laughing when Clint noticed two men enter the dining room. One was Detective Hocus, the other his partner.

"Looks like the police have arrived."

"I'm ready," she assured him.

Instead of waiting for the two men to spot them, Clint raised his arm and waved it until he caught their attention. Then he waved them over. He also caught the waiter's attention, and he reached the table just as the police did.

"Waiter, would you bring these two gentlemen some coffee cups and another pot of coffee."

"Of course, sir."

"Sorry to interrupt your dinner, Adams," Hocus said.

"You haven't," Clint said. "We've just finished. Sit down and join us for coffee."

Hocus sat and his partner walked around the table to take the other chair. Both men were studying Ruth.

"This is Ruth McDonald," Clint said. "These are Detectives Hocus and . . ."

"Wright," Hocus's partner supplied. "Pleased to meet you, miss."

The waiter came with the second pot of coffee and two extra cups, and Clint made a point of pouring the coffee for the detectives.

"Thanks," Wright said, picking his up and sipping it. Hocus ignored his and concentrated on Ruth.

"Miss McDonald, I'd like to ask you a few questions, if I may."

"Of course."

"Do you live in the city?"

"Yes."

"Where?"

"Five Points."

"Ah," Hocus said, not elaborating on what that meant. "Where were you last evening, Miss McDonald?"

"I was with Clint."

"For how long?"

"He came by Bogart's—that's a restaurant where I work as a waitress—and picked me up at closing time. That was about eight."

"And where did you go?"

"To my apartment in Five Points."

"How long did he stay there?"

"We both stayed there until about ten, and then we came here."

"Excuse me for asking, but how long did you stay here?" Hocus asked.

"I have no problem with these questions, Detective," she answered boldly. "I stayed here until morning."

"Was Mr. Adams with you all night?"

"Yes."

"How can you be sure."

"We *were* in the same bed, Detective."

"Couldn't he have gotten out of bed, left without your knowing it, and then returned later?"

"No."

"How can you be so sure?"

"Because when I'm in bed with a man I like to sleep wrapped around him," she said with no embarrassment. "I guess it gives me a feeling of security."

"I see," Hocus said, contriving not to look uncomfortable with his questions or her very frank answers.

"Is there anything else?" she asked.

"No, I think that will do it . . . for now. Oh, yes, where do you live?"

"On Mulberry Street," she said and gave him the address.

That was the first time it occurred to Clint that both Ruth's apartment and police headquarters were on Mulberry Street.

"All right, thank you both," Hocus said, standing up. He looked at his partner and said, "Let's go."

"I haven't finished my coffee yet," Wright complained.

"Let's go," Hocus said again, more forcefully.

Wright made a face, excused himself to Ruth, and as the two men were leaving they heard him say to Hocus, "Now can we get something to eat?"

"Did I do all right?" Ruth inquired.

"You did wonderfully," he said, taking her hand. "Tell me something, Ruth."

"What?"

"How far is your apartment from Police Headquarters?"

"About three blocks, I guess. Why?"

"I just realized that you live on the same street. That's all. Do you want some dessert?"

"Yes," she said, and as he raised his arm for the waiter she added, "but not here."

After a bout of dessert back in his room, they lay together on the bed, sated—for the moment.

"What happens now?" Ruth asked.

"What do you mean?"

"I mean, what are you going to do now? Leave New York? Or try to find your friend's killer."

"Ruth—"

"What was her name, anyway?" Ruth asked. "I can't keep referring to her as your friend."

"Her name was J.T. Archer."

"The one in the papers?"

"That's right."

"What was she doing writing novels?"

"I guess they paid better than the newspaper articles."

"Are you?"

"Am I what?"

She swore. "I think you're just being dense. Are you going to try to find out who killed her?"

"Yes."

"Did the police warn you not to?"

"Yes."

"But you're going to do it anyway."

"Yes."

She lay there for a few moments, wondering if she should scold him or try to talk him out of it, but instead she asked, "Can I help?"

"I think you can," he said.

"How?"

He took hold of her hand and said, "Put your hand right . . . there!"

The meeting between Tom Sadler and the killer was held in a Five Points alley. Just by coincidence—and perhaps an ironic one—the location was halfway between Ruth McDonald's building and Police Headquarters.

"I came from a dump like this," the killer said without preamble.

"Then why meet here?" Sadler demanded, scowling. "It's filthy, it's near the police—"

"It's good to go back every once in a while," the killer said. "You got my money?"

Sadler handed over an envelope. The killer counted it, then looked at Sadler curiously.

"There's more here than we agreed on."

"It's a standby fee."

The man frowned and said, "Another one?"

"It's possible."

"When will you know?"

"Soon."

"I can't wait forever."

"It'll be soon."

"Who will it be?"

Sadler's first instinct was to hold that back, but Kelly's orders had been to tell the man.

"Clint Adams," Sadler said, "the one they call—"

"The Gunsmith," the killer said. "I've done a lot of

work out west, too. I know who he is.''

''Will you stay?''

''Sure,'' the killer said. ''It might be interesting.'' He put the money in his pocket and said, ''It might be damned interesting!''

Ruth had not lied to Hocus about the way she liked to sleep, but halfway through the night she disentangled her limbs from Clint's, and he got out of bed without waking her.

He'd been waiting for the opportunity for hours because he had suddenly remembered something—the piece of paper he had picked up in J.T.'s apartment.

He went to his jacket, picked it up, and dug into his pocket. The paper had been crumpled, and had been squashed as a result of being carried around for so long. He opened it up and tried to smooth it out, and what he saw nudged his memory.

He lit a match so he could see better, and in the light he saw a sketch, a drawing in pencil of J.T. Archer's face— in death. The killer had taken the time to draw her picture after he killed her—and then left it behind! By accident?

What kind of man would kill a woman, and then take the time—wait a minute! It struck him then and he went to his bag and pulled out a piece of paper. He put the two pieces of paper next to each other on the dresser and, lighting another match, compared them.

He was no art expert, but the pencil looked identical, and both drawings appeared to have been done by the same hand. The drawing of the dead girl and the drawing that had been done of him by the man on the train! What was his name? Thatch, that was it. Adam Thatch!

Was Adam Thatch the man who killed J.T. Archer?

There was only one way to find out, Clint decided,

folding both drawings and stowing them in his bag, and that was to find Thatch.

The only problem with that was how to find one man in a city the size of New York when all you knew was his name—if that were his real name!

SIXTEEN

In the morning Clint and Ruth made slow, pleasant love. It was a fine way to start a new day. After a bath Ruth dressed for work, telling Clint that she had the morning shift that day and would be done before six.

"Maybe we can meet," she suggested.

"I don't know where I'll be, Ruth," Clint replied honestly, "but keep the key."

She smiled and put the key in her bag. If she hadn't been so enthusiastic about the sex they'd had, he thought, he might believe that she cared more for the bath and the food and the luxuries that the St. Nicholas afforded her and that she couldn't get in Five Points than she did for him. Even if she did, though, that would be okay. He never asked a woman to profess undying love for him.

She moved to the bed, where he still lay naked beneath the sheets. She slid her hand beneath his neck and passionately kissed his mouth and said, "Just something to remember me by while you go through the day."

"I'll remember!" he shouted as she ran out the door.

He stayed in bed staring into space, then got up to wash and dress. He'd been alternating his new suits up until now, but this time he dressed in some of his clothes that he'd brought with him. He slipped one of his own vests on over the shoulder rig and, although it was not as good a fit as the specially cut jacket, it hid the gun well enough from the eye of the casual observer.

With Ruth gone he pulled out the two drawings again and examined them in the daylight. He felt even more sure that they had been done by the same man, the one he knew as Adam Thatch. His only connection to this man was the tailor where he'd bought his suits, so he decided that that would be his first stop—after breakfast.

He was having breakfast in the dining room when a stocky, well-dressed man in his forties entered the room, looked about, and then approached his table.

"Excuse me, sir," the man said politely.

"Yes?" Clint said, looking up. Was this another detective? A man assigned by Captain Fletcher to watch him?

"Would you be Clint Adams?"

"That depends on who is asking."

"Forgive me," the man said, holding a bowler hat in his hands. "My name is Edward Zane Carol Judson."

"That's a mouthful, all right."

"Otherwise known as Ned Buntline."

Clint paused as he was transporting a piece of steak to his mouth, looked up at the man, and said, "Why don't you have a seat and join me for breakfast, Mr. Buntline."

"Please," the man said, "the name is Judson. Buntline is simply a byline." Nevertheless, he sat.

"Some breakfast?" Clint asked.

"Perhaps some coffee."

Clint signaled the waiter for another cup, and when Judson had a full cup, Clint asked, "How were you able to pick me out?"

"I got your description from Holman," Judson said. "The man is an abominable editor, but he described you very well."

"That answers that question," Clint said. "Now, why have you come to see me?"

"Well, in light of what happened yesterday to poor J.T.—it made the evening papers, and the morning papers again—I assumed that you would be coming to see me. I thought I would save you the trouble."

"That editor didn't believe I was who I said I was."

"He does now, I assure you." Judson sipped his coffee, then put the cup down, and said, "I am at your disposal, sir. Ask away."

"Any questions I had about you—that is, about Ned Buntline—were answered by that Holman character. You were not writing the dime novels I came to New York to put a stop to."

"No, I was not," he sighed, "but I wish I had. Miss Archer's writing was really very good, and her subject matter? Why, only the best I've ever encountered. I only hope that Holman will let me continue—"

"*Whoa* there," Clint said, cutting the man off. "I don't want more of those books written."

"But surely you can't be serious," Judson said. "There is so much information that was not used. Why, J.T.'s notes—"

"What do you know about her notes?" Clint asked. "The police have them."

"If I was to lend my name to her venture, surely she had to show me her notes."

"Why didn't you try to take the books over then?"

"Well, at the time I was not convinced that they would be a success."

"And what has made you change your mind?"

"Well—"

"Wait a minute," Clint said, frowning. "You've talked to someone in the police department, haven't you?

The only reason you want to continue the books is because I'm here in New York and someone told you that I'd be looking for J.T.'s killer.''

"You've caught me, sir," Judson—or was he truly being Butline now?—said. "In truth, I think that anything you do while you're here would make an even more successful novel than any of the ones J.T. has written to date.''

"Why?"

"Think of it, sir! A legend of the old west comes east to find the killer of one of his—ah—earlier friends. A true western legend stalking the streets and alleys of the largest city in the east. Why, the possibilities are unlimited.''

"Not as unlimited as you think, Buntline," Clint said. "The answer is no.''

"All I wish to do is accompany you on your investigation. I will merely observe your methods of detection—''

"I'm not a damned detective!"

"You are modest, sir. Some of J.T.'s notes outlined murders that you solved. She followed your career quite faithfully. Why, she was planning a novel called *The Black Pearl Tong* based on your recent escapades among the opium dens and whorehouses of San Francisco's infamous Chinatown.

"Look, Buntline or Judson or whatever you call yourself," Clint said evenly, "I had no intention of letting J.T. continue writing those books, and I don't intend to allow you to, either.''

Looking crafty, Buntline said, "I suppose the police would be very interested to hear you say that—''

A cold look from the Gunsmith cut him off.

"Not that I would tell them—''

"Don't try to brace me, book writer," Clint said menacingly. He was genuinely angry at the man's intimation of blackmail. "The pen may be mightier than the sword, but I don't carry a sword!"

"Yes," the writer said, "I see. Well, then," he went on, rising, "I'll leave you to your breakfast."

"If you haven't already ruined it," Clint said.

"If I have, I apologize," the man said, "and I wish you luck in the search for your friend's killer."

"Good day, Mr. Judson."

The man said, "Good day, sir," and replaced his bowler on his head.

Clint watched the man leave and wondered if the darn fool was going to try to follow him when he left. If he was, he and the patrolman Fletcher put on his trail would probably trip all over each other.

He hoped.

SEVENTEEN

After breakfast Clint left the hotel and walked to Broome Street, to Henry's Tailor Shop. He didn't bother to look back to see if anyone was tailing him, because there were plenty of reasons that he might be going to a tailor shop.

"Ah, Mr. Adams," Henry said, grinning happily, "I love when a customer comes back. You haven't—ah—used up those suits already, have you?"

"No, Henry, the suits are fine," Clint said. "Actually, I came back to ask you a few questions."

"Oh? About what?"

"About our mutual friend, Mr. Thatch."

"Mr. Thatch?" Henry repeated, frowning. "What about him?"

"Has he been in since I was here?"

"Why, no, I haven't seen him. I'm sure he will, though. He always stops in to do some business with me when he's in town."

"Well, would you know where he stays when he's in town?"

"I'm sorry, Mr. Adams," Henry said, "but I really don't ask my customers where they're staying, unless they ask me to deliver a suit. Mr. Thatch always picks them up himself, much the way you did."

That was true, Clint admitted. Not once had Henry asked him where he was staying.

"All right, Henry, I'll tell you what. I'd really like to get a hold of Mr. Thatch and buy him a dinner to thank him for sending me to you."

"Well, that's nice."

"Yes. I'm staying at the St. Nicholas, just around the corner. Now, if Mr. Thatch should come in for a suit, I'd appreciate if you wouldn't tell him I was asking for him."

"What is it you'd like me to do, then?"

"I'd like you to get in touch with me after he leaves and let me know when he'd coming back to pick up his suits. That way I can be here when he gets here, you see?"

"Yes, I see, but if you and Mr. Thatch are friends, Mrs. Adams, I don't see why you don't—"

"Henry," Clint said, taking a dollar out of his pocket and tucking it into the tailor's shirt pocket, "I thought you didn't ask your customers questions."

"I don't," the little tailor said.

"If you do as I ask," Clint added, "I just might come back and buy a couple more suits."

"It would be my pleasure to serve you, Mr. Adams," Henry said, taking the dollar out of his shirt pocket and transferring it to his pants pocket. "Yes, sir, my pleasure."

Clint left the tailor shop feeling disappointed. He had hoped that Henry would be able to give him a definite location for Thatch. If the man were the killer, would he stay in town now that his job was done? Would he endanger himself for a couple of new suits?

Then, again, why should he think himself in any danger? The police had no idea what he looked like, or that he had anything to do with J.T.'s death. The man could come and go as he pleased.

Clint thought that he probably should have let Buntline

accompany him and observe his methods of detection. He could just hear the stocky writer running along behind him asking, "Is that it?"

Yes, Buntline, damn it, that's it! Clint thought. I said I wasn't a damn detective!

The man who called himself Adam Thatch stepped out of the tailor's backroom as Clint Adams left, and the little man turned to face him.

"You were right," he said in an entirely different tone of voice than he had used in the presence of the Gunsmith. Now he sounded like a man totally sure of himself and not like a timid tailor at all.

"I'm always right, Henry," Thatch said. "You know that."

"Yeah, but how did you know?"

"Once I found out that the Gunsmith was in town, I realized that it was he I sat next to on the train. I've seen pictures of him, you know, and I'm ashamed to say that I actually sketched him and still did not recognize him."

"That sketching is gonna get you into trouble yet," Henry complained.

"It already has, Henry," Thatch said, although he didn't bother telling the tailor that he had dropped the sketch he had made of the dead girl, possibly right in her apartment. Whether in the apartment or on the stairwell, he assumed that if the Gunsmith had found it instead of the police, the first place the man would come was to the tailor shop, his only link with the man he knew as Adam Thatch.

"Look, I don't like this at all," Henry said, "you can't play games with this man like the others—"

"Henry," Thatch said, patting the man on the cheek, "just go on being my broker and my banker and not my conscience, all right?"

Henry's tailor shop was actually the killer's bank, and

his go-between, a way station by which potential clients could get in touch with him. Of course, the Gunsmith didn't know this and, in fact, Henry *was* an excellent tailor, which was why Thatch had recommended him to the stranger on the train. In point of fact, he sent a lot of customers to Henry for simple tailoring jobs.

"All right," the killer said, "here's what we're going to do . . ."

EIGHTEEN

"Excuse me?"

Clint looked at Justin, the desk clerk, and repeated his question. "Where does Boss Kelly live?"

"I, uh—"

"Come on, Justin," Clint said, "you live here, I don't. A man as big as Honest John Kelly—you must know where he lives."

"Uh—yes—I guess I do."

"Then you can tell me," Clint said, "because if you don't, somebody else will—" and Clint leaned across the desk so that his face was right in front of Justin's as he added, "Only I don't feel like asking anyone else, right now. Understand?"

Justin swallowed hard and nodded that he understood. Clint waited for him to decide what he was more afraid of, the prospect of John Kelly or the Gunsmith in the flesh.

"Fourteenth Street," Justin said, and gave Clint directions how to get there.

"Thanks, Justin," Clint said, patting the man on the shoulder and leaving him looking miserable.

How could he have known that Boss Kelly *wanted* to see the Gunsmith?

Before going to see Kelly at Tammany Hall, Clint once again stopped by the *Herald* building, presenting himself to the same woman who had directed him to the editor, Holman, on his last visit.

"Mr. Holman's office—" she began to say, recognizing him.

"I'm not here to see Mr. Holman this time."

"Well, Mr. Bennett is still out out of town, and Mr. Savitch—"

"Not them, either."

She frowned and asked, "Who are you here to see?"

"I'd like to take a look at some back issues of your newspaper."

"Oh, well, that's easy. For that you'll have to go to the morgue."

"The morgue?"

She nodded and said, "That's where they keep all the dead papers."

"How do I get there?"

"It's downstairs. Go out here and make a left, then walk all the way to the end until you see the stairwell. You'll have to go down and walk past the press rooms to get to it."

"The press rooms."

"That's right."

"Thank you, ma'am."

Clint followed her directions and went past the press rooms where three expensive presses were in operation.

When he reached the door to the room he wanted, he knocked and entered. An incredibly old man looked up from a desk and stared at Clint with watery eyes beneath a green visor.

"Can I help you?"

"I'd like to look at some of your back issues?"

"How many?"

"I don't know . . . about a year's worth?"

"That's a lot of newspapers, young fella," the man said. "Why don't you tell me what you're looking for and maybe I can help you find it?"

"I want to read everything you've got on Boss Kelly."

The old man stared at Clint for a few moments, then grinned, revealing a toothless cavern. It took Clint a moment to realize that the man was actually smiling.

"You gonna knock him off his pedestal?"

"What makes you think that?"

The old man shrugged a bony shoulder and rose slowly, as if standing up caused him great pain.

"You're a stranger in this city, or you wouldn't need us to tell you about Boss Kelly. I get the feeling maybe you been hired to knock him off his pedestal."

It took a few moments, but Clint finally realized that the old man thought he was in New York to kill Honest John Kelly—and the old timer approved of the idea.

"I'll tell you what, Pop," Clint said. "Why don't you sit back down and just tell me what you know about Boss Kelly?"

The old man paused, then sat his bones down, and said, "Why don't you go and get us some coffee, young feller, and give me a chance to collect my thoughts."

"You got a deal. My name is Clint."

"Mine's Grady, Clint. Now, you go right across the street and bring back a lot of it. These old bones need warming."

Clint retraced his steps and went outside. Directly across the street was a small restaurant, like many of the others in and around Printing House Square—only there was something different about this one.

There was a man standing in the doorway, a man Clint thought he recognized. As he started across the street toward the restaurant, the man's face became clearer until he was able to make out who it was. Lieutenant Dick Hoyt.

"Lieutenant," Clint said, joining the man in the doorway.

"Stopping for lunch, Mr. Adams?"

"Just picking up some coffee for a friend," Clint said. "Does Fletcher have you trailing me now?"

"Not really. I act on my own these days."

"Must be nice for you," Clint said. "Would you like some coffee?"

"Why not?"

Inside, as Clint was waiting for a pot of coffee to take across the street, he and Hoyt had a cup of coffee at a small corner table.

"What's on your mind, Lieutenant?"

"I'm just keeping an eye on you, Clint—and why don't you just call me Dick?"

"All right, Dick. What makes me so lucky?"

"Oh, I know how people react when they lose someone they like . . . or love."

"Oh? And how's that?"

"They tend to rush in without thinking . . . and get their heads shot off."

"I haven't gotten my head shot off in . . . oh, three or four days now, Lieutenant."

"Dick."

A waiter came with a pot of coffee and two cups and Clint stood up and paid him.

"I'll bring it back—" he started to say, but the waiter, who appeared to be almost as old as Grady, shook his head.

"I'll get it back from Grady. I don't know how he keeps gettin' fellas to come here to get his coffee for him. I keep telling him to sell his information for money, instead."

"Maybe he just likes to talk," Clint said.

"That's the truth."

"Thanks."

He turned and Hoyt stood up and blocked his path.

"Lieutenant, I appreciate your concern, but I would also appreciate your not getting in my way."

"Hey," Hoyt said, holding his hands up, "last thing on my mind, Clint. I swear."

"Sure. Pay for the coffee we had, will you?"

"My pleasure."

Clint left, reasonably sure that when he came back out of the *Herald* building, Hoyt would still be there.

NINETEEN

"What took you so long?" Grady asked as Clint returned.

"I met a friend," Clint said, setting the pot of coffee on the man's desk.

Clint poured two cups, then pulled a chair against the wall, sat back, and listened to Grady talk about Boss Kelly.

"He educated his brother and his sisters—and himself—and then he decided that he was going to go into politics."

"Early on," Grady continued, pausing to noisily sip coffee, "Kelly turned his attention to local politics, attaching himself to the Democratic Party. In 1853 he was elected to be an alderman, and in 1854 he was elected to Congress, defeating a man named Mike Walsh, one of the most notorious politicians of his day. He was reelected to Congress, and near the close of his term resigned his position, and was elected a sheriff of New York by a wide margin. In 1865 he was reelected to the same position.

"He's had some bad times," Grady went on. "His wife died in 1866, his only son in 1868, and his two daughters in 1870 and 1872. His own health got bad so he up and went to Europe, using the money he'd made in private business."

"Sounds like a resourceful man."

"He is. He came back in 1871, got back into politics, and eventually overthrew Boss Tweed and the Tweed Ring. Now, he's comptroller of the whole blamed city."

"So then, what's the bad side of Boss Kelly?" Clint asked.

"He's mean," Grady said. "He's suspicious of everyone, thinks they're out to get him, he's vindictive, and he'll do anything to keep what he has."

"Even murder?"

"I said anything. I don't think he's ever actually killed anyone, but you can always get somebody to do that for you."

"Who does he get?"

"He's got a toughie who works for him and takes care of his heavy work. Name is Tom Sadler. Now there's a mean one, and Sadler's probably the one Boss Kelly should be most suspicious of."

"Why's that?"

"Sadler's got ambitions of his own, and I wouldn't be surprised if he wasn't just using Boss Kelly as a stepping stone—or trying to. The Boss ain't nobody's stepping-stone, I can tell you that."

"How do you know so much?"

"Shit," the old man said, laughing until he was almost choking on it, "I was the best damned reporter until they dumped me down here just because I got a little old."

A little old, Clint guessed, was now somewhere around eighty.

"Well, thanks for the information, Grady," Clint said, standing up and putting his hand on his pocket.

"Don't come out of that pocket with no money," Grady said. "The coffee's good enough, and the chance to talk some is even better."

Clint withdrew his empty hand.

"Thanks again, then."

"Take some advice from me, young man."

"What's that?"

"Whatever you got in mind, just watch both Kelly and Sadler carefully. Even if Kelly wanted you alive, Sadler might want you dead and it would end up looking accidental." The old man's watery eyes bore into the Gunsmith's and he said, "Watch your back."

"Oh, that won't be a problem," Clint said, thinking of Dick Hoyt. "I've got somebody doing that for me."

Or he thought he did.

When he got to the street, he took a few moments to take some deep breaths and clear the dust out of his nose, but when he looked across the street, Dick Hoyt wasn't there. He looked around a bit without seeming to, but could not catch sight of the lieutenant.

The man was either very good—or he wasn't there at all.

That was all right. Despite what Clint had told Grady, he'd had people watching his back for him in the past, good men like Bat Masterson and Wyatt Earp, but that never stopped him from watching it himself, anyway.

His next move was up in the air until he finally decided to go to see Captain Fletcher for two reasons. Number one, he wanted to find out what Lieutenant Dick Hoyt was up to. Second, he wanted Fletcher to allow him to go into J.T. Archer's apartment on Sutton Place.

He didn't know what he'd find—or even what he was looking for—but it was basically for want of something better to do.

After all, what he'd told Buntline was true. He'd had some luck in the past, but that didn't make him a damned Pinkerton detective, just somebody who wanted to find out who had killed a friend of his.

It was ironic, he thought, that when he first met J.T. Archer in Leadtown, that's exactly what he was trying to do.

We've come full circle, J.T., only you aren't here to see it.

TWENTY

Patrolman Swan once again drew the duty of showing Clint to Fletcher's office. Idly Clint wondered what exactly Patrolman Swan's actual duties were.

"What do you want, Adams?" Fletcher asked impatiently.

"Just to ask a few questions, Captain," Clint said, standing before the man's desk. "As a matter of fact, you might even call them favors."

"Favors?" Fletcher said, looking up in surprise. "You're here asking for favors?"

"It doesn't hurt to ask," Clint said, frowning.

Fletcher scowled and rubbed his face, then said wearily, "All right, go ahead. Ask."

"I'd like to be able to go into Miss Archer's apartment on Sutton Place."

"What the hell for?"

"Sentimental reasons."

"I've had you checked out, Adams," Fletcher said, "and I hadn't heard that the Gunsmith was sentimental."

"You're not a man who believes everything you hear, are you, Captain?"

"The girl have any family?"

"No. Her father died years ago."

"You claiming to be the only family?"

"What?"

"The only way I can let you in to clean up her effects is if you claim to be her only living family."

"All right, then. I am."

"That mean you'll pay for her funeral?"

"I said that before, didn't I?"

"I'm just making sure," he said. "I guess that entitles you to go into her apartment." Fletcher opened his desk drawer, pulled out an envelope, drew a key from it, and said, "Here's the key."

Clint took it, frowning. "You had this in your drawer all along? Were you expecting me?"

"If I was, that would make me pretty smart, wouldn't it? And if I was smart, would I be in this job?"

Clint decided that the wisest course of action was to allow that question to go unanswered.

"Is that all?" Fletcher asked.

"No, not quite," Clint said, pocketing the key. "I want to talk to you about your man Hoyt. He and I had a talk this morning and—"

"Wait a minute. Who did you say?"

"Hoyt, Lieutenant Hoyt. I saw him today—"

"Was this the first time?"

"No, I saw him the other night at my hotel."

"What's he look like?"

"You don't know what your own man looks like?"

"Humor me, Adams."

Clint described Lieutenant Dick Hoyt in detail, right down to his ingratiating manner.

"I want to know what his job is," he went on. "I mean, is he going to be following me? A lieutenant? That seems a waste of man power, doesn't it?"

"Look, Adams," Fletcher said, "I don't know who this fella Hoyt, is, but he sure as hell isn't a lieutenant working for me."

"What? But he showed me a badge—"

"Badges aren't hard to come by, Adams," Fletcher said. "I know every lieutenant on this force and I'm telling you we don't have any Lieutenant Hoyt. Now get out of my office!"

TWENTY-ONE

The Gunsmith went back to the St. Nicholas Hotel and took up position at a corner table in the St. Nicholas bar to ponder the information he'd just received from Captain Fletcher.

There *was* no Lieutenant Hoyt on the police force, so who was the man who claimed to be Dick Hoyt? Of course, there was no reason that couldn't be his real name, but what his game was—that was another story.

There had been no sign of the man outside the *Herald* building, nor on the way to police headquarters on Mulberry Street. Likewise, as Clint returned to the St. Nicholas, he did not see Hoyt on the street or in the lobby.

Before repairing to the bar, Clint had asked Justin about the man.

"You remember the man who wanted to see me the other night?"

"Yes, sir," Justin said, having acquired respect for the Gunsmith since his arrival in New York.

"You ever see him before then?"

"No, sir."

"You don't know who he is?"

"No, sir, I really don't. He simply asked me to point you out when you arrived and to tell you that he wanted to talk to you."

Justin was eager for the Gunsmith to believe him, and Clint Adams did.

In the bar, Clint worked slowly on a beer while he pondered his next move. As if he didn't have enough problems trying to find Adam Thatch, now he had an unknown quantity thrown in for good measure.

Dick Hoyt.

Thinking the situation over, Clint decided to consider the possibility that it was Hoyt who had killed J.T. and was now playing a cat-and-mouse game with the Gunsmith.

So there it was. He was faced with a two-fold problem, dealing with two men he knew little or nothing about, Adam Thatch and Dick Hoyt.

"I cannot believe that you need my help," the Countess said to the man Clint Adams knew as Adam Thatch.

"Please, Countess," Thatch said, appreciatively eyeing the woman across the table from him. "Please, don't misunderstand. I don't *need* you so much as I choose to use you."

"Use me?" she asked, raising her dark eyebrows. In point of fact, everything was dark about the Countess except for one thing—her skin. She had midnight black hair and eyebrows, and she affected solid black clothing. Even the lip gloss that she wore was dark, albeit dark red. Her skin, however, was different. Her flesh was alabaster, and in sharp contrast to everything else, it made her mysterious, alluring, and a challenge to any man who saw her.

"Use me?" she said again to the man across the table. "How could you, a man, use me? Haven't you heard, darling, I use men."

"Precisely," Thatch said, "why I have come to you. I want you to be the queen in my newest game of chess, Countess."

"You're playing chess now—what name are you going by now, dear?"

"Thatch."

The Countess wrinkled her nose at that, but continued, "I thought your games were much more dangerous than that."

"Countess," Adam Thatch said, raising his wine glass to his lovely dinner companion, "with you as my queen, chess is the most dangerous game of all."

"Darling," she said, raising her own glass, "after that, how can I refuse?" They both drank, and then the Countess leaned forward with undisguised eagerness and said, "Tell me, who is the opposing king?"

Clint Adams was still in the St. Nicholas bar—which was like no saloon he had ever been in in the west—when a woman walked in. Apparently, women were not a rarity in New York bars, but this was no ordinary woman. As soon as she walked into the room, every man there was in her power—the Gunsmith no exception.

She was tall, full-breasted, and seemed to glide rather than walk. She had beautiful long black hair that reached—incredibly—almost to her ankles. Her clothing was also black. Her gown reached down to her ankles and was cut deep between her two full, well-rounded breasts. Her skin, however, was what arrested the eye, because as black as everything else was, her skin was as pale as alabaster. Add to all of this a slash of dark red on her mouth, and the end product was devastating.

The woman stood just inside the door and seemed to be searching the room. All of the men there stood up straight, slicked back their hair, sucked in their stomachs, did everything they could to attract her attention, but her eyes simply slid right over them, by them—in some cases, through them—until they fell on a man sitting at a corner table. He had been described to her with artistic detail and she recognized him immediately.

The Gunsmith.

"I've come for you," she said, standing before his table like some sort of apparition from a dream—a beautiful apparition!

She had glided across the room to his table and he had made every effort not to let her see him watching her while trying to do just that peripherally.

"What?" he asked. Then aware that he should have said something more intelligent, he said, "Pardon me?"

"I've come for you," she said again, as if it should have made perfect sense to him the first time.

Up close the effect of her skin, her hair, and her style of dress were even more devastating, and Clint was suddenly aware that Ruth might be waiting for him in his room. Ruth, who for all her wonderful qualities, would become invisible if she were to stand in the same room with this woman.

"I'm afraid I don't—" he said, afraid that he might be coming across as unduly dense.

To her credit she exhibited unlimited patience.

"You are a stranger in New York, are you not?" she asked and, for the first time, he became aware that he could hear some kind of an accent in her speech, which he could not identify.

"Yes, I am."

"You see, that is obvious. It is also obvious that you need a guide to show you the sights."

"The sights?" he asked. "It's very late—"

"That is the time to see New York," she said, "or any

city. The night, my dear, is the most exciting time of day!''

She extended her hand to him and said simply, ''Come.''

To his surprise he found himself putting his hand out for her to take. Then he stood to leave the St. Nicholas with a woman whose name he did not know and who he could not even have claimed to have met yet!

TWENTY-TWO

First she showed him Broadway, explaining to him that it was to New Yorkers an exciting hub of activity.

He said, "Other than San Francisco this is really my first time in what you would call a large city."

"Really?" she said. "I would not have thought so. You seem so . . . worldly."

"That word is often confused with cynical."

"You see," she said, "you are worldly."

Broadway, she explained, was the heart of New York, and the people were its life's blood. They flowed in and out of it, keeping it pulsing and alive.

They started at the St. Nicholas and strolled north, passed a theater. At the corner of Prince Street, on the east side, was a spectacular brownstone hotel, in the rear of which was another theater.

As they continued north, Clint was surprised at how many people there were on this particular thoroughfare.

"Doesn't this town ever close down for the night?"

"Never," the woman replied, linking her arm through his.

"How far are we walking?" he asked.

She stopped so that they were standing in front of the mammoth Grand Central Hotel and said, "I thought perhaps this far."

He looked at her and her face seemed to glow where the moonlight touched it.

"This is my hotel."

"Who are you?" he asked.

"It's better this way," she said, taking his hand and drawing him toward the entrance of the hotel. "No names, no identities to get in the way."

"But—"

She touched his mouth with her left hand, the scent of her subtle perfume tickling his nostrils. He had not even been aware of it until she touched the fingers of her hand to his mouth, and now there seemed to be a cloud of it around his head. It was a heady, almost dizzying scent.

"Later," she said, "later we can talk."

She pulled and he resisted. She moved in closer to him then so that her body was touching his, setting him on fire.

"You're not going to tell me you don't want to."

"No," he said, and then as she tugged him toward the hotel entrance he thought, Hell, no!

In her room he watched as she removed her dress. Even her underwear was black, and when she removed it he caught his breath. Her breasts were full and round and firm, and her nipples were large and pale. The hair between her legs was as black as the hair on her head.

"Do you like it?" she asked teasingly.

"Sure do," he said truthfully.

"Show me, then," she invited, shifting her bare feet so that her legs parted. She put her hands on her hips and said, "Show me."

He almost did, and then he caught himself. It was obvious that this woman was used to getting her way with men, and she had chosen him out of all the men in that bar because she thought she'd be able to get her way with him.

Well, he had two options. He could turn around and walk out and leave her there—which would probably be a novelty for her—or he could show her that she had made the wrong choice.

And leaving didn't appeal to him at all.

He began to undress, slowly, so that she was forced to wait for him, and as she waited she looked. He watched her eyes and when his erection came into view, full and throbbing, he saw approval in her eyes, which she quickly masked.

When he was fully naked, he approached her and, close up, could feel the heat her body radiated.

"Show me," she said again, licking her lips. "Kiss me."

"I'd love to kiss you," he said, moving closer to her. She closed her eyes and tilted her chin up, but instead of kissing her, he began to lick her red lips.

"Wha—" she said, before he muffled her by rubbing his lips over her mouth, removing the heavy lip gloss she was wearing.

"First, we have to get rid of this!" he said sensuously.

He slid one hand around her, holding her tight while he cleaned the garish red from her full lips. He was acutely aware of the feel of her naked flesh against his hand, his thighs, his penis as it pressed against her belly.

Finally, he released her and she fell back, going down to one knee and staring at him. She couldn't understand why he had done that.

"What are you doing?" she demanded, touching the back of her hand to her mouth.

"What I'm not doing," he said, "is not playing your game. Instead," he said, stepping forward, gripping her by the upper portion of her arms and pulling her to her feet, "we're going to play mine."

''What do you think—'' she started to demand, but he brought her to her feet and kissed her—hard! She resisted him, tried to push away, but the hold he had on her was firm. His fingers tightly held her arms, but suddenly she didn't care about that. All she cared about was his mouth on hers and the feel of his penis prodding her body.

She reached between them and grasped his penis in both hands, and when he released her, she went to her knees and began to lick the length of his shaft. Moaning, she cradled his balls and took his penis fully into her mouth. She was marvelously skillful and in a moment she had him near bursting.

''Wait,'' she said, reaching for her and pulling her to her feet again. This time, though, he brought her to the bed. She lay there on her back, watching him.

''Go ahead,'' she said.

He growled, ''When you want me.''

She licked her lips and then said huskily, ''I want you.''

He knelt on the bed and palmed her breasts. As he had surmised, they were firm, firmer than Molly's but not as firm as Ruth's. They were larger than Ruth's, though, and he hefted their weight in his hands. He moved his hands so that her rigid nipples were in his palms, and then he slid his hands down her body until his fingers were probing her fully.

She was slick when he found her and his fingers slid easily.

''Oh, God,'' she moaned, arching her back. Not wanting to waste any time he quickly slid down and replaced his fingers with his mouth. He licked her, flicked at her, and burrowed his tongue deep.

She arched her back even more, like a taut bow, and cried out, ''Oh, God, yes, that's it, yes . . .''

He teased her and then backed off, then teased her again until she said, "Now, more, please."

She reached down to grip the back of his head with surprising strength and hold him there. He pursed his lips around her and flicked at her with his tongue, drew on her and sucked on her until she was bucking beneath him wildly, crying out something he couldn't understand . . .

Then he was inside her, his cock seeming to swell even more, filling her, as he worked himself in and out of her. She reached around him, wrapping them in a blanket of her hair, clinging to him, meeting every thrust of his hips with a thrust of her own until finally they stopped. He began to fill her, each spurt causing pleasure for him, unbounded pleasure for her as she matched his orgasm with her own of equal intensity.

"What's your name?" he asked later.

"Call me the Countess."

"Are you?"

"What?"

"A countess?"

"Actually," she said, "yes, I am."

"But what's your name?"

She took a deep breath and said, "The Countess Angelina Margarita de la Fortuna."

He turned his head so that he could look at her and said, "I'll call you Angel."

"If you must call me something," she said, staring at the ceiling, "I would prefer Angela."

"All right," he said, "Angela. I don't have such a fancy name, just Clint Adams."

"Clint."

"Yes."

"I think you had better leave now."

"Really?"

"Yes, really."

"Why?" he asked. When she didn't answer, he asked again, "Why, Angela? Because I wouldn't play your game?"

"Yes, that's why," she said, not looking at him. "You did something to me that no man has ever done. I—I need time to think about that."

"All right," he said, getting up from the bed and dressing. She didn't speak while he dressed and as he walked to the door he said, "You know where I am."

"I know."

He thought about saying good night, but decided against it and simply left.

The smile on her face was like that of a cat who has just devoured a very tasty canary.

As Clint entered his hotel room, he knew he'd made a mistake. He didn't have time to ponder it, though, because Ruth was waiting for him, wearing a towel.

"Not much to do when you're not around except take baths," she explained.

"I'm sorry I'm late."

"There's no reason to apologize," she said. She dropped her towel and slowly—knowingly—got dressed.

"Ruth—"

"I told you I'd be here until you found someone better, Clint," she said. With that unerring instinct that women have, she knew that he'd been with another woman. "I guess now you have."

"No," he said as she moved past him to the door, her clothes sticking to her damp body, "not better."

"I know," she said, smiling at him lamely, "just

different.'' Then she used the same exit line on him that he had used on Angela. "You know where I am.''

After she left, he knew where he was. Alone.

He gimmicked the doors and windows so that he would be alerted if someone decided to try to break in, and then he went to sleep.

TWENTY-THREE

In the morning the Countess rose and prepared for her bath. Afterward she stood in front of her mirror and examined her pale body.

Clint Adams had left slight marks of passion on her upper arms. Absently, she rubbed her hands over them, remembering how his body had felt, the things he had done to her with his mouth, his tongue, his manhood. He was quite a man and would probably be quite an adversary.

Things had not gone totally as she'd expected them to go the night before. He had not reacted as most men did, but had instead reacted by seeking to impose his will on her. She had been surprised by this, but allowed him to do so because the end result was the same.

They had tasted each other, and she knew that he would want more.

Oddly enough, she realized that—and this was somewhat disconcerting—so did she.

Clint awoke the following morning with a new outlook on what had happened the night before.

It was not a rarity for him to go to bed with a woman shortly after meeting her, but this one time did not sit right with him. There were too many other possibilities to be considered, the major one being that she had been sent after him by either Thatch or Hoyt.

But why?

Certainly not to kill him. She could have done that easily enough at several different times during the evening, or one of those men could have waited for them in her room—or in a darkened doorway—and done it alone.

Of course, there was the possibility that she was supposed to have killed him and for some reason had been unable to. He was not foolish enough to think that it might have been his sexual prowess that changed her mind but, in light of how they had spent their short time together, what else could it have been?

Then there was the third possibility: She had been sent in to evaluate him because he was as much an unknown quantity to Thatch or Hoyt as they were to him.

Whatever the case was, that she had simply walked into the St. Nicholas bar and been captivated by his good looks did not sit right with him, so he decided that she had some ulterior motive in taking him to bed.

The only way to find out what it was, was to see her again, and if she felt that he was coming back simply because of her effect on him . . . well, she was only partially right!

"What did you find out about him?" Thatch asked the Countess later that day.

The Countess frowned, as if the light of day bothered her. Her best time was night, and she felt uncomfortable being out and about during the day. She was also uncomfortable with the thoughts she'd been having all morning, thoughts about Clint Adams, thoughts she'd never had about a man before.

"Not very much."

"Why not?" Thatch asked, eyeing her speculatively. "Don't tell me he . . . resisted your obvious charms? No man's ever been able to do that, right, Countess?"

She smiled across the table at him and said, "Hardly."

"How well I know it," Thatch said, although he also knew that a man couldn't get near the Countess unless she wanted him to.

"He's a strong-minded man with a will of his own, Thatch," she answered shortly.

"Now, that's nothing I couldn't have guessed at, Countess," he said. "I hope you're not going to be a disappointment to me on this."

She frowned at him and said, "That sounds suspiciously like a threat."

"Will you be seeing him again?" he asked her, ignoring her remark.

She sat back in her chair, maintaining her calm facade while inside she was shuddering. If the man who was calling himself Adam Thatch during this trip to New York were threatening her . . .

Thatch was a funny man. She knew that he wanted her, but she also knew that he wanted her on his terms. That was why she refused to let him have her. He was a dangerous man, however, possibly the only man she'd ever been afraid of.

The Gunsmith, though. Now there was a man she could be afraid of. She had allowed *him* to have her last night on his terms and had almost convinced herself that it was only to achieve her end—Thatch's end. As the day went by, though, she was not so sure.

"I'm sure I will," she said, with more confidence than she felt. If indeed he did not return, it was going to be a new experience for her, one she would have to deal with.

It might mean that she was getting . . . old.

"Pay more attention this time," Thatch instructed her, looking thoughtful, "I want to know all I can about Clint Adams—the Gunsmith—before I sweep him from the board."

"You mean, before you try."

He looked at her sharply and for a moment she thought that perhaps she had gone too far.

"He impressed you," Thatch said after a moment. "Countess, a man impressed you?"

"That's not so rare, Thatch," she replied. "You impress me."

"Yes, but I'm special," he said immodestly. "Are you trying to tell me that Clint Adams is special?"

"You asked me to find out a few things about him," she replied. "How special he is, that's something that you're going to have to find out all by yourself."

"Oh, I will, Countess," he assured her, smiling. "I will, indeed."

TWENTY-FOUR

Clint decided that Captain Fletcher might be able to tell him something about the Countess. He doubted very much that she was a real Countess. More than likely she was a woman who knew how to get what she wanted from men without telling them what it was. A lawman like Fletcher might know about a woman like that.

He knew there was a chance that Fletcher wouldn't see him, but he decided to try. It would pass the time until he went looking for Angela, after making her wait most of the day for him to show up.

A different patrolman showed him to the captain's office this time.

"What happened to Swan?"

"He's sick," the man replied without turning around.

After the patrolman announced him, he waited to hear the captain's voice shouting for him to get out, but instead the patrolman stepped aside and said, "The captain will see you."

"Thanks."

"Sit down, Adams."

Clint sat and frowned at the man behind the desk.

"I expected you to kick me out."

"I might have, but I'm thinking that maybe we can help one another."

"Having a problem finding a killer?"

Fletcher scowled and said, "Nobody in her building or around it saw anything. The man who killed her was a professional. He came, did his job, and went without being seen. That kind of man is not going to be easy to find."

"So?"

"I was thinking about the man you told me about. What was his name? Boyd?"

"Hoyt."

"Yeah, Hoyt. Could he be the killer?"

"If he was, why would he be tailing me *before* he killed the girl?"

The question surprised him as much as it did the captain. It had not consciously occurred to him, but Hoyt was in the hotel lobby waiting for him the night J.T. was killed.

"He could have killed her after he saw you."

"He could have, but why stop in to see me? And for that matter," he went on, gathering steam, "if he had been to see her, she didn't know I was in town."

"So what's your point?"

Clint shrugged and said, "I don't know what my point is, Fletcher. I'm just trying to work this thing out."

"You're not helping," Fletcher said, frowning. "You might as well leave."

"How about letting me ask one?"

"All right," Fletcher said. "One."

"You know a woman called the Countess? Otherwise known as Angelina Margarita de la Fortuna." Clint started to describe her, but he could see by the look in the captain's eyes that he knew who she was.

"Angie Fortune," Fletcher said. "So she's playing the Countess again, huh?"

"Then she is a fake?"

"Actually, she's not," Fletcher said. "I mean, she's a real countess, but all she's got is a title that she got from some poor sap who married her years ago. She was going to take him for all he had but he upped and died on her before she could get to it."

"So she's rich?"

Fletcher laughed.

"Her husband the count left all of his money to his mother. She didn't get a cent."

"How can she afford to stay in a hotel like the Grand Central?"

"Don't be naive, Adams," Fletcher said, and then he looked sharply at Clint and said, "Or maybe you're not. Maybe you don't see many women like her where you come from."

"Maybe not," Clint said, just to keep the man talking.

"Well, she's probably got some man paying her bills, Adams, hoping to get . . . Never mind. Why are you asking me about her?"

"Oh," Clint said, getting to his feet, "somebody mentioned her to me, told me to watch out for her. I just wanted to find out more."

"Well, whoever told you that gave you good advice. As far as con women go, she's the very best."

Clint didn't doubt that for one second. "All right, Fletcher. If she comes after me, I'll remember."

"Come after you?" Fletcher said derisively. "Angie Fortune—the Countess—has got better taste than that, Adams. You can't afford her."

"No," Clint said, heading for the door, "I don't suppose that I can."

As he reached the door, he turned with his hand on the knob and said, "Oh, by the way . . ."

"Yeah?"

"If you need any more help, let me know."

"Get out of here!"

When Clint got outside, he was surprised at who he saw standing right across the street.

Dick Hoyt.

He crossed the street and the man stood there, waiting for him.

"Man impersonates a lawman," Clint said, "it's not exactly the smartest thing to be doing, standing right across from Police Headquarters."

"Fletcher tell you he didn't know me?"

"He told me," Clint replied. "Was he telling me the truth?"

"As much as he knew," Hoyt said, "but let's not talk about it here, Clint. Can I buy you some breakfast?"

"I had breakfast."

"All right, I'll buy you an early lunch, then."

"Okay."

"In a better part of town, if you don't mind."

"I don't mind at all, Hoyt."

TWENTY-FIVE

They ended up at the St. Nicholas, sitting in the dining room with Hoyt devouring a huge lunch while Clint satisfied himself with coffee.

"You want to tell me who you are?" Clint asked.

"My name is real enough," Hoyt said. "It was just my profession that I hedged on a little."

"Hedged?"

"I'm not a duly appointed lawman," Dick Hoyt admitted, "but I am a lawman of sorts."

"Pinkerton?"

Hoyt nodded.

"Why are the Pinkertons interested in me?" Clint asked, not sure for a minute that the man was telling the truth this time either.

"We're not," Hoyt replied, "but we are interested in the man who killed Miss Archer."

"You were here before you knew she was dead."

Hoyt's eyes caught Clint's and he shook his head.

"You knew?" Clint asked, staring at the man. "You knew she was dead when you came here to see me that night?"

"Yes."

"How?"

"I went to see her," Hoyt answered, "and found her that way."

Holding his anger in check Clint asked, "Did you report it?"

"No," Hoyt said, shaking his head. "I knew the police would find out sooner or later."

"So what brought you to me?"

"Maybe I'd better start this a little earlier on," Hoyt suggested. "We're working for Bennett."

"James Gordon Bennett," Clint said, "the owner of the *Herald*?"

Hoyt nodded.

"He's in Europe."

"He contacted Pinkerton from there," Hoyt explained. "He's been having his paper sent to him there, and when Miss Archer started her series, he started to fear for her life, so he got in touch with us."

"She got killed while you were bodyguarding her?"

"Don't jump to conclusions, Adams," Hoyt said with steel suddenly in his voice. "If I was guarding her, she'd still be alive, but the woman wouldn't be guarded. She absolutely refused."

"Stubborn," Clint said, remembering that about J.T. Archer.

"You've got that right. She also told me that if she were going to have a bodyguard, it would be you. We checked her background and found out she knew you."

"That doesn't explain how you knew I was here," Clint said, digging further for reason to believe what this man was telling him.

"I was watching the train station and recognized you. I also recognized someone else."

"Thatch?"

"Who?"

Clint explained about the man he had been sitting next to on the train, about the connection he'd made because of the matching sketches.

"Describe him."

Clint did so, in detail, while Hoyt listened, nodding his head.

"His name's not Thatch," Hoyt said. "It's Stillman—at least, we think that's his real name. It could be any number of names he's gone by, but we're reasonably certain that it's Stillman."

"You know him?"

"Enough to have recognized him at the station."

"Why didn't you follow him?"

Looking embarrassed, Hoyt admitted, "I lost him in the crowd." When Clint didn't comment, the man continued, "I went to Miss Archer to tell her that a hired killer was in town and that he was probably here for her. At the same time, I recognized you and told her that you were here. She said she'd get in touch with you."

"You didn't lose me in the crowd?"

Hoyt studied Clint for a few moments to see if that was some form of criticism and then, apparently satisfied by what he saw, said, "No, I followed you here."

"All right, let me get this straight, then," Clint said. "You knew that a killer was being hired?"

"We heard there might be. I was at the station to see if I could recognize him when he got off the train—if he got off the train. I was surprised to see you—"

"How did you recognize me?"

"Got a photograph of you from a Washington contact. I assume you've done some work for the government?"

"Once or twice."

"Well, that explains that."

"Why didn't you tell me who you were that first night?"

"My original plan was to keep an eye on you in case the killer tried for you."

"Why would you think he might?"

"If you and Miss Archer were as close as our reports said you were, I figured you'd want to find out who killed her. Stillman wouldn't leave New York knowing that someone of your reputation was looking for him. His ego wouldn't let him."

Thinking about Angela, Clint asked, "Would he send someone to check me out for him?"

"He probably would. Why?"

"I'd just like to be alert."

Hoyt frowned, but Clint went on before the man could ask any further questions.

"What are your plans now?"

"The same," Hoyt said, "to keep watching you. I just thought that if you knew about it, we might have a better chance."

"Maybe we will."

"What have you been doing to find him?"

For some reason, Clint had been expecting this question ever since Hoyt had told him that Thatch was really Stillman.

He wasn't prepared to answer it because he still wasn't absolutely sure whom he was talking to.

They took the discussion into the St. Nicholas bar and continued it over a couple of cold beers.

"You don't believe me, do you?" Hoyt asked.

"You've lied to me before."

"I could show you some identification."

"You showed me a badge."

"Oh, yeah," Hoyt said. "Well, maybe you can accept the fact that I'd like to get to Stillman. There's a price on his head in most of the eastern states."

"Pinkertons are allowed to accept rewards?"

"Why not?" Hoyt said. "We can use the extra change."

Clint shrugged the question aside.

"Has he ever operated in the west?"

"Once or twice," Hoyt said, "but I don't think you would ever have heard of him."

Clint took a sip of his beer.

"Adams? Do you have anything to tell me that might help me find him?"

"Dead or alive?"

Hoyt frowned and said, "I'm not a bounty hunter."

"You're not a lawman, either. How do I know you didn't kill her?"

"Me? Why would I—"

"I don't know," Clint said, leaning forward to stare intently at the man. "Maybe everything you've told me is true, except for one thing."

"Like what?"

Watching the man intently for his reaction, Clint said, "Maybe you're Stillman."

"Then who's the man on the train?"

Clint shrugged and said, "Maybe he's just a man who likes to draw pictures."

"Yeah, and maybe you're a policeman," Clint said sarcastically.

"Hey, you can't forgive one little lie, can you?"

Clint put his beer down so hard that it spilled on the

table and the floor. He stood up, and although he felt like shouting, he spoke in a low, even tone that wouldn't draw attention to them.

''You knew she was dead that night you came here and you played games with me,'' he said tightly. ''I don't care who you are—that's not something I can just shrug off.''

''Adams, I didn't know who I was talking to—''

''You still don't,'' Clint said, walking away, ''and neither do I.''

Clint went back to his room to cool down, have a bath, and then dress for the Countess. He was convinced now that she had been sent to him the previous night for one reason or another—and tonight he was going to find out what that reason was.

TWENTY-SIX

It was getting late and Clint Adams had not shown up yet. Angela Fortune—alias, Angelina Margarita de la Fortuna—moved to her mirror again to study herself absently while wondering if this Gunsmith was waiting for her to come to him.

Thatch or no Thatch, she thought, that would be one hell of a wait.

Clint walked through the lobby of the Grand Central Hotel as if he belonged there, hoping that no one would stop him before he got to the steps.

He was wearing his dark suit.

Nobody stopped him.

Upstairs he found the Countess's room and knocked on the door.

She answered, wearing a dark, filmy nightgown that showed off her breasts to their best advantage.

"I don't want to see you—" she started to say, swinging the door shut. He stiff-armed the door and it snapped out of her hand, slamming open.

"Hey!"

He moved his arm, pressed his hand against her chest, and guided her to the divan in the center of the room. She fell on to it with a flash of white thighs.

He then went and slammed the door hard enough to shake the wall.

It was then he realized how angry he was at the man who called himself Dick Hoyt, and he was going to take it out on her.

"What the hell—" she started to say, trying to get to her feet.

"If you get up I'll just sit you down again."

She sat back down, staring up at him, and very deliberately covered her thighs with her gown.

"You're a real gentleman."

"And you're a real phony," he said. "I was going to play along with you, Angela, but not anymore."

"I don't know what you mean."

"Sure you do," Clint said, sitting on the divan. "Thatch, or Stillman, or whatever his name is, he sent you to check on me, to find something that he could use."

"Like what?"

He shrugged and said, "A weakness?"

"Like what?" she asked again.

"Like you, maybe," he said, reaching over and uncovering her thighs. "Like your fair white skin."

"Are you saying my fair white skin doesn't appeal to you?" she asked coyly. "That's not what it seemed like last night."

"I told you, Angela," he said. "No games."

"Clint, I don't understand—"

"Look, honey," he said, "I know what you're up to, so it isn't going to work. I just want you to know that, and I want what's his name to know that, too. All I want you to do is tell him that."

She frowned and asked, "That's all?"

"That's all."

"You . . . don't want me to tell you where he is?"

Clint laughed at her and said, "Sweetheart, you don't know where he is."

"How do you know that?"

"Because he's a professional. Nobody knows where he is but him."

She frowned at him and said, "What about you?"

"What about me?"

"Are you a professional?"

"Sure."

"But not like him."

He put his hand out to her to help her up, and when she took it, he pulled her to her feet.

"Am I like him?"

She thought a moment and then, searching his face, said, "No, you're not."

"All right," he said, removing his jacket, "now we can go to bed."

Afterward he asked, "Is your name really Angela Margarita de la Fortuna."

"Actually," she replied, "it is. I was born Angela Trout—isn't that awful—and then I married Ricardo de la Fortuna while he was visiting this country from Spain. He died soon after and left me with even less than I had before I met him."

"You seem to be doing all right now?"

"This?" she asked, laughing. "I can't pay for this, Clint. I only got the damn suite because of my title. I've got to stay here until I can figure out some way to pay for it."

"You think Thatch, or Stillman—what do you call him?"

"This trip I call him Thatch."

"Do you think he'll pay you enough to pay your bill?"

"Whatever he pays me will help," she said, "but that's not even worth thinking about now."

"Why not?"

"Now that you know—"

"Well, he doesn't know that I know," Clint said, interrupting her. "Tell him whatever you want."

She frowned, propping herself up on one elbow and looking down at him.

"You don't want me to set him up for you?"

"Would you, if I asked you to?"

"No."

"What if I offered you a lot of money to do it."

"That would be a different story," she admitted.

"Well, I don't have a lot of money," he said, taking her hand, "all I have is this." He pulled her hand down and put it on his cock. She closed her hand over it, stroking it, and it immediately began to swell.

"That's not enough for you to betray him, is it?"

"No," she said, moving down so that her mouth was near his erect penis, "but we can start with this and see what we come up with—oh, it's up already!"

As her lips closed over him, taking him inside her talented mouth, he wondered who she thought was fooling whom.

TWENTY-SEVEN

When the Countess met Thatch the next morning, she knew that she could tell him just about anything, so she decided to tell him the truth. Clint Adams seemed more than prepared to handle him.

"He came to my room last night and told me that he knew that you had sent me."

"Is that right? Did you even bother to deny it?"

"I did."

"What did he do?"

"He got very forceful."

"That was very gentlemanly of him," he said, "but then, what would you expect from a westerner? What did he do after that?"

"He took me to bed."

"Really?"

"Look, you can believe me or not, that's your choice," she said, starting to rise.

"Relax, Countess, relax," Thatch said. When she sat back down, he told her, "I didn't say I didn't believe you."

"Well, you act like it."

"Here," he said, taking an envelope from his inside jacket pocket and sliding it across the table to her. "Would I be paying you if I didn't believe you?"

"No, you wouldn't," she said, reaching for the envelope. As she closed her hand over the envelope, his hand suddenly came down and caught hers in a powerful grip that belied his size and slimness.

"What would I do, Countess, if I thought that you were lying to me?"

Unsuccessful in trying to free herself, she blinked back tears of pain and said, "You'd kill me."

"That's right," he said, staring directly into her eyes, "I'd kill you."

He released her hand and she snatched it to her lap before he could grab it again. She didn't rub it. She'd do that after she left him.

"Now," he said, smiling pleasantly, "give me your honest evaluation of this man."

"He's tough, smart," she said, standing up, "and probably too much for you to handle."

He leaned back and smiled at her, shaking his head.

"You're very brave in a room full of people, Countess," he said in mock admiration.

"I don't think I want to see you anymore . . . Stillman," she said. She turned her back on him and strode toward the door, her shoulders hunched, prepared for anything.

If she had been looking at him, she would have seen him react to the name Stillman as if she had slapped him in the face.

Once outside, the Countess became just plain Angie Fortune, hurrying down the street in an attempt to get as far as she could from Stillman before he could decide to come after her.

She had probably made a poor decision, she knew, but she seemed to have managed to ally herself with the Gunsmith—at least, in Stillman's eyes.

She only hoped that Clint Adams was half as good as his reputation said.

• • •

Thatch—or Stillman—briefly considered going after the Countess but then decided against it. She could still be useful to him in the near future.

As for Adams, he seemed to have come across some pretty dangerous information. Thatch had not thought that anyone knew about the name Stillman. He was going to have to find out from this Gunsmith how he had gotten that information—before he killed him.

Clint Adams was waiting in Angela's room when she got back from her meeting with the man he had come to think of as Stillman.

He was seated on the divan in the center of the sitting room, and she stared at him for a moment before speaking.

"How did you get in here?"

He had originally left that morning at the same time she did and had gone back to his hotel to change his clothes.

"This may be a big, expensive hotel," he replied, "but the desk clerk still responds to a little bribery."

"You've been here the whole time?"

"Sure."

"You didn't follow me?"

"You know the city better than I do, Angela," he told her. "Could I have followed you?"

"I don't think so."

"So, what did you tell him?"

"I told him, uh—"

"The truth, right?" Clint asked. "That I knew he sent you, and that his name—one of them, anyway—is Stillman. You told him what we did last night?"

She put her hands on her hips and glared at him.

"You knew I'd tell him all of that, didn't you?" she demanded.

"I figured that was the worst you could do," he said, uncrossing his legs.

"I don't understand you."

"What else did you tell him?"

"I told him he probably couldn't handle you—although I don't know how true that is."

"That's all right," he said, standing up and reaching for her, "neither does he."

"Wait a minute," she said, dancing back out of his reach, "wait a damn minute."

"What's the matter?"

"You don't trust me."

"Did you tell him the truth?"

"Well, yes—"

"Should I have trusted you?"

"Well, no—" she admitted sheepishly.

"If it's any consolation, Angela, I know you didn't do it to hurt me," he told her. "I know there was nothing personal in any of this."

"Well, there wasn't!" she snapped.

"I know that," he said again. "I know you were just trying to pay your hotel bill."

"Pay my bill?" she said, looking at him like he was crazy. Was that really the only part of her story he'd believed? "I've run out on bills in better places than this."

"Well," he said, apparently distressed, "guess I just wanted to believe that there was some good in you. I guess I was wrong, huh?"

She stared at him, believing him for a moment, and then as a slow grin spread over his face, she said, "Oooh, you—" and swung her fist at him. He ducked; she missed and twirled completely around before falling on her ass.

Clint stared down at her and said, "And you can't fight worth a damn, either."

TWENTY-EIGHT

When Clint returned to the hotel, he found a message waiting for him at the desk. In fact, he found a few messages, all handed to him by Justin, the desk clerk, who never seemed to be off duty.

"I'd like to send a telegram, Justin," he said, accepting the messages.

"Sure," Justin said, eager to please. He took out a piece of paper and, poised to write, said, "I can take care of that for you."

"For a price?"

"Uh, well—"

"That's all right," Clint said, "I'll pay you—but it better get sent."

"Oh, it will. I promise."

Clint decided that it would. Justin was apparently a very enterprising lad, and if he wanted Clint to use him again—for anything—he'd make sure the telegram got through.

Clint quickly dictated a short message to Rick Hartman in Labyrinth, Texas, requesting as prompt a reply as possible. Justin read it back, and Clint was satisfied that he had it right.

"One more thing, Justin."

"What's that, sir?"

"I wouldn't take very kindly to it should someone else get a look at that."

149

"Of course not—"

"No matter how much they offer you," Clint went on. "It just wouldn't be healthy for you."

Justin gaped at him for a few moments, then said, "I understand."

"Good."

Clint turned his back and briefly considered reading the messages there in the lobby, but finally decided to return to his room first.

The first message was from Ruth, simply asking when she would get a chance to see him before he left. Feeling guilty, he momentarily set it aside.

The second message came from Dick Hoyt, requesting a meeting. Without any guilt whatsoever, he set that one aside also.

The third message was from the tailor, Henry, asking Clint to come to his shop as soon as he could. As much as he would have liked to respond to that one immediately, Clint recognized that both Dick Hoyt and Angela had distracted him from another visit he had meant to make much earlier, the visit to Tammany Hall.

He tucked Henry's message into his jacket pocket, vowing to follow up on it after he paid a visit to Honest John Kelly—the Boss.

Clint admired the headquarters of the Tammany Society as he mounted the steps leading to the front door. He used the brass knocker to knock and waited patiently for an answer. It would take a while in a building that size.

He was about to knock again when he heard the sound of a door opening from within. Apparently, just inside this main set of doors there was another, inner set. In seconds, the outer door was opened and he was facing a tall, slender man with hostile eyes.

"Good afternoon," he greeted. "I would like to see John Kelly, please."

The man frowned at him and said, "And who are you?"

"My name is Clint Adams."

He thought he detected a flicker of recognition in the man's eyes, but to the man's credit it was quickly masked.

"What's the nature of your business?"

"Personal."

"I don't think Mr. Kelly knows you—"

"Excuse me, but who are you?" Clint asked, annoying the man with the interruption.

"My name is Tom Sadler," he finally replied. "I am Mr. Kelly's executive assistant."

"Well, why don't you just run along like a good assistant and tell him I'm here. I'm sure he'll see me."

"I don't think so—" Sadler began, closing the door.

Clint put his foot in the door, forcing it back open so hard that it almost struck Sadler in the face and would have had he not jumped back. This allowed Clint to step into the small foyer.

"I'll wait here."

Sadler matched stares with the Gunsmith, came up second best, and fled through the second set of doors. Clint closed the main door behind him and settled down to wait at least one or two minutes. Anything more than that and he'd simply walk in.

He actually gave the man five minutes, at which time he returned and said to Clint, "Please follow me." Apparently, Kelly had agreed to see Clint, and this did not sit well with Sadler.

He followed Sadler through a large sitting room, into and through what appeared to be a meeting room of some kind, and finally to a closed door upon which Sadler knocked, and then opened.

"Clint Adams," he said, stepping aside to allow Clint to enter.

The man behind the desk rose and regarded Clint critically, appraising him.

"This is John Kelly," Sadler said.

Kelly was a tall, slender man whose shoulders were somewhat wider than those of his assistant. The other difference was in their faces. Where Sadler's eyes were hostile, Kelly's were positively guileless—and not to be believed in a politician.

"Come in, Mr. Adams," Kelly invited good-naturedly. He looked at Sadler and said, "That'll be all, Tom."

"Boss—"

Kelly threw him a look and for a moment his face changed completely. What Sadler saw in it pursuaded him to leave them alone.

Clint moved forward and Kelly said, "Have a seat." After Clint had obliged, Kelly asked, "Are you one of my constituents, Mr. Adams?"

"I'm not even from New York, Mr. Kelly," Clint said, "but then you already know that?"

"I do?" Kelly asked innocently. "And just how would I know that?"

"You're Boss Kelly, aren't you?"

Kelly smiled and said, "I've been called that, yes."

Clint closed his eyes for a moment, trying to hold himself in check. He was still angry at Dick Hoyt and had not yet found an outlet for that anger.

"Mr. Kelly, I'd rather not play games."

"I'm afraid you have me at a disadvantage—"

"I'll tell you what," Clint said, interrupting the smooth politician, "why don't I talk and you listen? After I'm finished, you can go on pretending you didn't know what I was talking about, but I won't have to stay here to listen to it."

Kelly frowned then and said, "Suppose, Mr. Adams, I simply have you put out of my office, since you seem to harbor some hostility toward me?"

"If you tried that, Mr. Kelly, your nice office would end up getting all messed up. You wouldn't want that, would you?"

Kelly stared at Clint for a few moments, then sat back in his chair, and simply said, "All right, then. Talk."

"My message is very brief," Clint said. "J.T. Archer was a friend of mine. You know who she was, don't you?"

"Of course. I read the papers. She's the newspaper-woman who was killed."

"Right. My only message to you is that if you had anything to do with her death, I'll be coming after you."

"Me?" the man snapped, looking outraged. "Why would I have anything to do with her death?"

"She was speaking out against you rather loudly in print," Clint pointed out.

"And it was her right to do so. I see, now. You think I had her killed because of what she wrote about me. You're all wrong on that, Adams—"

"If I am," Clint said, standing up, "then you've got nothing to worry about, do you?"

"Wait a minute, Adams," Kelly said, standing. "I can't have you running around town claiming I had some-one killed. I am, after all, in the public eye."

"What do you suggest?"

"Well," Kelly said, "I could make some sort of a donation to your favorite charity—"

"That sounds good," Clint said, and before Kelly

could react he said, "You send the money to Captain
Fletcher at Police Headquarters. Tell him you're paying
for J.T. Archer's burial."

"And you won't keep asking—"

"I'm asking questions whether you pay or not, Kelly,"
Clint said. "I just figured that since you were feeling
guilty enough to offer me a bribe, you might want a
outlet—"

"Guilty?" Kelly shouted, slamming his fist down on
the desk. "For what? Look, Adams, I can make life pretty
hard for you here in New York—"

"Good," Clint said, grinning tightly at the politician
who had finally lost his cool outer shell, "that's what I
was hoping for."

Clint turned, strode toward the door, and stopped as it
opened and Tom Sadler stepped in.

The Gunsmith turned back to Kelly and said, "You
take your best shot, Boss Kelly, and I'll take mine." He
walked right past Sadler, through the house, and out the
front door.

"Boss?" Sadler said, looking at Kelly.

Kelly was standing behind his desk with his fists
clenched, almost shaking with rage.

"You get in touch with your man from Chicago,
Tom," he said through clenched teeth. "That is a dangerous man, and I want him out of the way." He emphasized
his point by slamming both fists down on his desk and
shouting, "Now!"

TWENTY-NINE

From Tammany Hall Clint went directly to Henry's tailor shop. As he approached it, he saw that the curtains were drawn, even though it was still early evening.

He opened his jacket to give easy access to his gun. He became aware of a nagging thought that had been playing in the back of his head—that Henry was more than just Stillman's tailor. A hired killer needed someone to act as a bridge between him and his clients, and Henry would have fit that bill perfectly. His shop was a perfect front.

Only now, the front seemed to be closed.

Clint approached the front door carefully, turned the knob, and found the door unlocked. Aware that he could have been walking into a trap, he preferred to think that he was not. A man like Stillman wouldn't ambush him. He'd take him on right out in the open. His ego wouldn't allow him to do otherwise.

No, if anything, this visit was going to bring across some kind of message, and the only way he was going to find out what it was, was to go inside.

Hand poised to snatch at his gun, he opened the door and entered slowly.

The place was a mess. There was clothing strewn all over, and equipment—and Henry.

The tailor was in the center of the room, barely visible beneath a pile of clothes that seemed to have been deliberately piled atop him.

Still cautious, but positive that he and the tailor were alone, he moved to the center of the room, toppled the pile of clothing, and examined the body.

He had been stabbed once, cleanly. The work of a professional. He was about to stand up when he saw a piece of paper protruding from the dead man's pocket. He grasped the edge of the paper, pulled it out, and smoothed it.

It was a drawing, but instead of a portrait it was a cartoon, the kind used for commentary in a newspaper. It depicted two men, one of whom was obviously Henry; the other was the man who had been sitting next to Clint on the train.

Stillman.

That wasn't all, though. The Stillman figure was driving a knife into the chest of the figure of the tailor. The pain etched on the face of Henry was so real that Clint could almost feel it.

There was one line of dialogue written at the bottom: You're fired!

Stillman had fired his go-between in the most permanent way possible, thereby sending the Gunsmith a message.

If he would kill Henry, a man who had been of some use to him, he would surely kill Clint Adams, a veritable stranger. All he was probably waiting for was the word from his employer, the man who had hired him to kill J.T. Archer.

And Clint had the feeling that, after his visit to Boss Kelly, that word would not be long in coming.

After Clint left Tammany Hall, Tom Sadler left and, through a prearranged signal, met with the man he knew as Adam Thatch.

"You can go ahead," Sadler said.

"And do what?" Thatch asked.

Sadler paused, and then said, "You know."

"Why is it that men like you can hire men like me to kill people, but you can't say it?"

Sadler looked stubborn, then frowned and said, "All right then, you can go ahead and make arrangements to kill Clint Adams."

The killer smiled and, thinking of his former associate, Henry, said, "I've already started."

Thatch turned to leave, but Sadler called out and said, "After that, I might have another job for you."

Thatch looked at Sadler and knew, as he had known all along, that the man was a flunky for someone else. It looked now as if the flunky were about to turn.

"We'll talk about that," he said, "after the Gunsmith."

Clint left the shop and went back to his hotel. He decided against notifying the police himself because the last thing he needed was more trouble with Captain Fletcher. He left the sketch behind, tucked safely inside Henry's pocket, and went back to his hotel to figure his next course of action.

Actually, the next move probably wasn't his, at all.

It was Stillman's, and he was fairly sure that it wouldn't be made with a sketch.

He was wrong.

THIRTY

The next morning the police showed up at the hotel and knocked on Clint's door. He staggered out of bed to the door in his longjohns and opened it to Detective Hocus and his partner, Detective Wright.

"What?" he asked, squinting at them.

"Did we wake you?" Hocus asked.

"Yeah," Clint said, rubbing his hand over his face. "What do you want?"

"Captain Fletcher would like to speak with you."

"Now?"

"No," Hocus said, looking Clint up and down, "you can get dressed."

Clint turned his back to them, reaching for the same pants and shirt he'd worn the night before. As he reached for his gun, Hocus said, "You won't need that!"

Clint turned to stare at Hocus and said, "I don't even sleep without it."

"You won't need it."

"I always need it."

"Not this time."

Clint turned to face the two detectives squarely, the shoulder rig in his left hand. Instinctively, both detectives shrank back.

"We are going to have one hell of a start to this day if you're going to insist on this," he explained. Staring at them, he very deliberately donned the shoulder rig, then reached for his jacket, and shrugged into it. He pulled on his boots, then stood up, and said, "Let's not keep the captain waiting."

As they left he had no doubt that this had something to do with the murder of the tailor.

"We found this in his records," Fletcher said, handing a slip of pink paper across the desk to Clint. He accepted it and studied it. It was a copy of the receipt for his suits, and it had his name clearly written on it.

Handing it back to Fletcher, he said, "So?"

"Are you going to tell me that this is a coincidence?" Fletcher asked, putting the receipt down on his desk.

"I needed some new clothes."

"Why did you go to this particular tailor?"

"He was recommended to me."

"By whom?"

"A man I met on the train."

"What was the man's name?"

"Adam Thatch."

"Thatch," Fletcher said to himself, frowning. He didn't know the name.

Up to this point no one had mentioned how the tailor had been killed. Clint knew that this was an attempt to see if he would give himself away by mentioning a stabbing.

"Do I get to find out how this man was killed?"

Fletcher looked at him and said, "I thought you might already know."

"How would I know?"

"Never mind," Fletcher said. "He was stabbed, the same way Miss Archer was."

"Is that what this is about?" Clint asked, feigning

surprise. "You think he was killed by the same man who killed her?"

"It's possible."

"Do I understand that I'm a suspect?"

"That's nothing new," Fletcher told him. "You have been all along. I only have your word that you and Miss Archer were friends and that you didn't see her before she was killed."

"And my motive?"

"You didn't like the stories she was writing about you."

"What about the stories she was writing about Boss Kelly?" Clint asked. "Did he like them?"

"I told you to forget Boss Kelly!"

"He's not a suspect?"

"Adams—"

"All right, then what would my motive be for killing this tailor? I didn't like the cut of my suit?"

"Speaking of the cut of your suit," Fletcher said, and then looking at Hocus and his partner he said, "This man is wearing his gun."

Fidgeting nervously from one leg to the other, Hocus said, "He wouldn't give it up."

"Is that a fact?" his superior said, glaring at him and his partner.

"Don't blame them," Clint spoke up. "Going out without a gun is an invitation to getting killed for a man like me, Fletcher. It would have taken more than two of your detectives to take it away from me."

Fletcher stared at Clint for a few tense moments and then said, "I'm going to let the business about the gun pass, Adams, because I don't really think that you killed the girl."

"Thanks for the vote—"

"Don't thank me. I just don't think that a knife is your style. Now get out of here."

"You woke me up for this?"

"If you want more, Adams," Fletcher growled, "I can arrange it."

"No, that's all right, Captain," Clint said, standing up, "I don't want to impose on your hospitality."

He started for the door, then stopped and turned around to face the three policemen.

"What is it?" Fletcher demanded.

"I thought I'd tell you that I spoke to that man again, Dick Hoyt, the one who was pretending to be one of your lieutenants?"

"And?" Fletcher asked, annoyed.

"He claimed to be a Pinkerton."

"You don't believe him?"

"He lied once; he could lie again."

"We'll check with the Pinkertons."

"Oh," Clint said, returning to stand in front of the desk, "I've already done that."

He took out one of the telegrams he had collected at the desk the night before and gave it to the captain. It was from Rick Hartman who, through some of his contacts in Denver, had already checked on Dick Hoyt's story about being a Pinkerton agent.

"According to this," Fletcher said, "he *was* a Pinkerton, but was let go months ago."

"That's right," Clint said.

"It doesn't say why, though."

"I guess you can go ahead and find that out for yourself, Captain. I'm satisfied knowing that he's not a Pinkerton now."

Fletcher started to hand the telegram back, but Clint

held up his hands, saying, "Oh, you can keep that, Captain. I hope it helps."

"It tells us who he was," Fletcher said, dropping the telegram on to the desk next to the tailor shop receipt, "not who he is now or what he wants. I'll still have to get in touch with the Pinks."

Clint shrugged and said, "I can't do everything for you, Captain, can I?"

Clint could feel Fletcher's murderous glare on his back as he walked out the door.

THIRTY-ONE

On the street Clint touched his breast pocket, where the second part of Rick's reply was. He had requested that Rick reply in two parts, one concerning Dick Hoyt, and the other about a man called Thatch or Stillman.

The second telegram referred to the man as Stillman, a killer for hire who had a phenomenal success rate. He was a legend throughout the east, with only occasional forays into the west. According to Rick's telegram, there were too many descriptions of the man to be able to pick one out as correct. Still, the reply had told Clint what he wanted to know.

For years the Gunsmith had been annoyed by his reputation, but Clint knew for a fact that most men enjoyed the notoriety, especially men like Stillman, whose egos relied on their reputations.

There was no danger of Stillman's striking at him from behind or from ambush. His play would be made from the front. He had assumed this last night at the tailor shop, and Rick's telegram had cinched it for him.

All he had to do was wait for Stillman to do the eastern equivalent of calling him out into the street.

It was to happen sooner than he expected.

When Clint returned to the hotel this time, there was a message waiting for him at the desk. Justin constantly seemed to be the bearer of news for him, and this time the clerk was so excited that he forgot himself and lapsed into his Five Points accent.

"Mr. Adams, you ain't gonna believe who just left you a message," the desk clerk said excitedly.

"Who, Justin?"

"A countess!"

"Really?"

"I didn't know you knew a countess," Justin said, as if they were great friends who had never kept secrets from each other.

"I'm sorry, Justin," Clint said, "it slipped my mind. Can I have the message?"

"Sure, sure," Justin said. He turned and took a long brown envelope out of Clint's box and handed it to him. "Gee, what a beauty!" he said, his eyes shining.

"Don't be silly," Clint said, "it's just an ordinary brown envelope."

"But—" Justin started, but by that time Clint was on his way to his room. He didn't open the envelope until he was inside.

It was a sketch. He knew that the moment he took it out, even before unfolding it. He could tell by the type of paper. It was one of Stillman's sketches—only it was more than that. Stillman was calling him out.

He smoothed the sketch without smudging it and laid it on the bed.

For a moment he couldn't make any sense of it. At first it looked like a wall with a platform above it, but on second glance it looked a little like a bridge—or half a bridge—but unlike any bridge he had ever seen before.

What did it mean? The meaning was not readily apparent, so he continued to study the sketch until his head started to ache.

He needed some breakfast.

●   ●   ●

During breakfast he propped the sketch up against something so that he could continue to study it, but breakfast was over and he still wasn't sure what Stillman was trying to tell him.

A slim young waiter wearing glasses came with his second pot of coffee and Clint stopped him before he could leave.

"Look at this," he said, pointing to the sketch.

"Yes, sir," the waiter said, peering at it obediently.

"What does it look like to you?"

"That's the East River Bridge."

"The East River—" Clint began, then stopped. "It doesn't look like any bridge I've ever seen before."

"It's not finished," the waiter said. "It's gonna be a suspension bridge and when it's done it will connect Brooklyn and Manhattan."

"Where the hell is Brooklyn?"

"Across the East River," the waiter said, as if he were speaking to a child.

"All right," Clint said, deciding that where and what Brooklyn was had little to do with anything. "Tell me where this is," he said, tapping the sketch.

The waiter looked at it again.

"That tower is located on the river shore near the foot of Roosevelt Street."

"Tell me how to get there."

The waiter gave Clint instructions.

"Will there be anything else, sir?"

"No," Clint said, taking out some money and handing it to the man. "Thank you."

"What about the man and the woman, sir?"

Clint looked at the waiter.

"What man and woman?"

"The ones under the bridge," the waiter said, pointing.

Clint looked closely at the sketch and sure enough, beneath the bridge were these two minute figures—drawn in surprising detail, which made it obvious that they were a man and a woman.

"Why didn't I see that?"

"I don't know."

The woman seemed to be menaced by the man, and Clint asked the waiter if he saw the same thing.

"Yes, sir. Uh—could I ask you, sir, what this is supposed to be?"

"I think," Clint said, "that it's supposed to be an invitation."

"An invitation?" the man said. "Under the bridge, at night?"

"At night?" Clint asked, frowning.

"Well, it's obvious from this shading across the sky that this scene is supposed to be taking place at night."

Clint stared at the man and asked, "What are you, an artist?"

"As a matter of fact," the waiter said, "I do sketch a little."

That explained why the man had seen so much more in this particular sketch than Clint had been able to. The dark, broad lines across the top of the scene had meant nothing to him, but now that the waiter mentioned it, it did tend to make the whole scene look as if it were taking place at night.

"All right," Clint said, "thank you again."

"You're welcome, sir."

"Hey, what's your name?"

"Terry Beatty."

"I appreciate your help, Terry."

"Any time."

As the waiter walked away, Clint looked at the sketch one more time. It was all very obvious now. The man under the bridge was Stillman, and he was inviting Clint to meet him there to save the woman.

But who was the woman?

THIRTY-TWO

Clint went to the Grand Central Hotel to see the Countess, Angela Fortune. His first instinct was that she was the woman depicted under the bridge.

It didn't take him long to find out that he was wrong. She answered his knock as if she were just standing on the other side of the door waiting for him. She was wearing some sort of dressing gown that looked wrinkled, her hair was a little mussed, and she looked nervous.

"Did you get the message?" she asked as she let him into her room.

"I got it," he said. "What I want to know is where you got it?"

"It was left in my box, with a note from . . . from him, saying that I should give it to you," she explained, rubbing her upper arms as if she were cold. She was feeling a chill, all right, but it wasn't from the weather.

She was obviously afraid.

"I would have given it right to you, but you weren't in, so I left it."

"Did you see what it was?"

"I did; I looked," she said. "It's a sketch of part of the East River Bridge."

"Do you know what it means?"

"No," she said. Then she frowned at him and said, "What does it mean?"

''Why did you bring it to my hotel?'' he asked, ignoring her question.

''The note—''

''You could have burned the note, and this,'' he said, holding up the sketch.

''I . . . couldn't.''

''You're afraid of Stillman?''

She paused a moment and then replied in a barely audible voice, ''Jesus, yes. He'd just as soon kill me as look at me. I know that!''

This was not the same woman who had lured him from his hotel to hers the other night. That woman was calm, serene, infinitely confident. This woman was just frightened—hell, she was scared out of her wits.

Clint looked off to his left, through the doorway to the bedroom, and saw her bags on the bed, partially packed.

''Well, when I'm finished with him, you won't have to be afraid of him anymore,'' he said, ignoring the apparent fact that she was leaving.

''What does the sketch mean?'' she asked again.

''What do you see?'' he asked, handing it to her.

She took it, studied it, and said again, ''One of the towers of the East River Bridge.''

''And beneath it?''

She frowned, looked again, and then lifted her dark eyebrows in surprise.

''There is something beneath it, isn't there? It looks like . . . a man and a woman?'' She looked up at Clint and asked, ''Stillman?''

''Obviously.''

''Then he's challenging you to meet him beneath the bridge?''

''At night.''

"To rescue this woman," he said, pointing to the two little figures.

"But . . . who is she?"

"I thought she was you," Clint said, "which is why I came here, but now I think I know who it is."

"Where are you going?" she asked, as she headed for the door.

"Since we got the sketch today, it's pretty clear that he wants this showdown to take place tonight," he explained. "I want to try to get to the woman before he does."

"But what if he already has her—" she called, but he was out the door, leaving it wide open behind him.

He didn't know how Stillman knew about her, but he had to try to get to Ruth McDonald before the killer did.

First, he checked Bogart's, the restaurant where she worked, but she wasn't there. The owner told him that she had been due in, but never showed up.

He rushed to her apartment in Five Points next. When there was no answer to his pounding at her door, he kicked it in, splintering it in the process. She was not there, and there were definite signs of a struggle. He looked around in the event that another sketch had been left behind, but there was none. What he did find, however, were some drops of blood on the floor. He hoped that they were Stillman's and that the fiery Ruth had gotten her Irish up and raked his face open.

Clint cursed himself because somehow Stillman had found out about Ruth, either by following him or by talking to somebody else who knew.

Like Justin, the enterprising desk clerk at the St. Nicholas.

His first instinct was to go to Justin and wring his neck, but he had no doubt that the clerk had given up the information for money. Going after him was pointless.

He could also have gone to Fletcher and brought the police into it, but that might have gotten Ruth killed. No, instead, he was going to have to go after Stillman underneath the East River Bridge, after dark, just the way the man wanted him to.

He was going to have to face the man at a *place* of his own choosing, at a *time* of his own choosing. Every experience he'd ever had told him that wasn't the way to do it.

He knew he had to, though—and he had to find some way to even the odds.

"Why are you doing this to me?" Ruth McDonald asked the man who had dragged her out of her apartment just hours before. "What have I done to you?"

"You haven't done anything to me, young lady," Stillman replied, dabbing at his bloody cheek with a cloth. "At least, you hadn't until this."

"I'm sorry," she said, although she really wasn't, "but you frightened me."

"Yes, I'm sure."

They were in a room not far from her own in Five Points, one that the man had apparently rented for this specific purpose.

"Can you tell me what we're waiting for . . . please?" she asked.

"We're waiting for dusk, my dear," he said, "and as darkness falls on this great city, we will take a ride to the East River to take a look at that incredible bridge they're building there."

"Why do you want me to look at the bridge with you?"

she demanded, straining behind her back at the bonds that held her tight. "I don't understand."

"We have a meeting there, Miss McDonald."

"With who?"

"With a friend of yours— Clint Adams. He is a good friend of yours, isn't he? In spite of the fact that he has apparently lost interest in you?"

Frowning, Ruth asked, "What has Clint Adams to do with this?"

"Everything," Stillman said, folding the cloth and putting it away. The cut on his cheek had finally stopped bleeding. "You see, the Gunsmith's legend will come to a close in the shadow of that great bridge."

"You're going to kill him?"

He smiled, took out his knife, and, staring at the finely honed edge, replied, "Exactly."

Clint spent the rest of the day in the hotel, having lunch, waiting in the bar, having dinner, hardly tasting anything he ate or drank. He simply wanted to be where he could be found in case Stillman changed his plans.

Clint felt tremendous guilt over Ruth McDonald's involvement in all this. The woman certainly didn't deserve to have her life threatened simply because she had enjoyed a few nights of pleasure with him. And then he had practically cast her aside when Angela Fortune came into the picture. He was able to half convince himself that the reason for that was not Angela's beauty and sensuality, but that he had felt that she'd be able to lead him to J.T.'s killer.

He doubted that he'd be able to convince Ruth of that—but even before he could try, he had to get her safely away from Stillman.

As darkness began to fall, he went back to his room to

dress for his showdown with Stillman. He put on the clothes he had been wearing when he first arrived; then he fixed the shoulder rig and cut-down .45 for his gunbelt and modified Colt. If he were going to meet a man who apparently was not only a professional but a master, then he had to go in wearing his best chance on his hip.

That was the only way he had been able to think of to make sure the odds were at least even.

With his gun on his hip, he suddenly felt more comfortable than he had felt all during his stay in New York. He knew that when this was over he was going to head back west where he belonged. Born in the east, the Gunsmith had lived most of his life in the west, and this visit east told him that he was a westerner through and through.

Now all he had to do was get out from under that East River Bridge alive.

As Clint Adams left the hotel and walked toward the railroad that would take him to the East River Bridge—or pretty damn near it—he was so intent on Stillman, and on the safety of Ruth McDonald, that he was unaware of the man who stepped out of the shadows across the street and followed him.

The man had his hands stuffed into his pocket, and his heart was racing with anticipation. He was sure that this was it, what he had been anticipating for so long.

Clint Adams was going to lead him to the elusive Stillman—and maybe the Gunsmith would even help collect his bounty for him.

THIRTY-THREE

The East River Bridge was to be constructed in five parts. The central span over the river would be 1,595 feet long when it was completed. There would be a span on each side—the New York and Brooklyn sides—from the tower to the anchorage, 940 feet in length. Then there were the approaches on each side.

The portion of the bridge that was to be used as the meeting place was that area beneath the approach from the terminus to the anchorage. The streets below were crossed by stone arches at an elevation sufficient to leave the streets totally unobstructed for travel.

The scene depicted in the sketch which Clint Adams was carrying took place somewhere in this stretch at the base of one of the stone arches.

It was incredibly dark out, Clint noticed, because there were clouds in the sky hiding what was almost a full moon. Clint stared at the clouds, as if willing them to move and let the light through, but he gave up after a few futile seconds.

The Gunsmith had to take a moment to take a look at the partially completed East River Bridge. The tower itself was huge and imposing, and across the river there was supposedly one just like it. Between them right now was just open air, but eventually the two would be joined together. He shook his head, wondering what would happen the first time someone set foot on that bridge.

It had to fall. It would be just too damn heavy—wouldn't it?

Returning to the business at hand, Clint knew why Stillman had chosen this particular place to meet. Obviously, he would have familiarized himself with it earlier so that the darkness would be to his advantage. Also, his choice of weapon—the knife—would be most effective in the dark. Clint's choice of weapon, on the other hand, was rendered almost totally useless—and not by accident—because he couldn't see to shoot—at least, not until his eyes became used to the heavy darkness.

He wondered if Stillman would even give him that much time.

"I'm sorry about the gag," Stillman told Ruth McDonald, who was bound hand and foot, but propped against one of the pillars.

"I'll remove it soon enough," he promised, adding to himself, Just as soon as I spot this living legend I'll let you call him right to his death.

At that moment, Stillman heard something, peered through the darkness with eyes that were long used to it, and glimpsed an outline he assumed was the Gunsmith.

"Okay, my dear," he said, reaching for Ruth's gag, "it's time to start the party."

Ruth McDonald changed her mind several times within a ten second span.

First, she had decided to call out for help as soon as her gag was removed, but she then realized that she would be calling Clint to his death.

After that, she decided to keep silent even after the gag

was removed, making her captor go after Clint himself, without her help.

Third, she decided once again that she would shout out as soon as her gag was removed, but that she would call out to Clint to run and leave her there.

As Stillman removed the gag, however, he was too clever and cruel for her. She felt the blade of his knife bite into her side, and she screamed!

The scream echoed through the stone arches, bouncing about so that Clint could not successfully pinpoint a location. He did not panic, however, and rush in to try to find Ruth—which is what he assumed her scream was supposed to make him do.

"All right, Stillman," he called out into the darkness, "I'm here, but I'm not rushing in because of one little scream. You'll have to try something else."

He hoped that Stillman wouldn't decide to make Ruth scream again. What he was hoping was that the man would abandon the tactic and try something else entirely.

After a moment Stillman's voice came back at him from the darkness.

"We're here too, Adams," Stillman shouted. "Me and your little gal friend."

His statement was punctuated by another scream, this one a little more drawn out than the last. The first had been a scream of surprise, but this one was of pure pain.

"Let the girl go, Stillman," he shouted. "Now that I'm here you don't need her."

"I don't know about that, Adams," Stillman called back, his voice echoing. "I might have some use for her after you're dead. I've been known to need a pretty woman after I'm finished with a job."

Suddenly, Clint was able to discern shapes. He could see some of the pillars as darker outlines against the ordinary black. He still couldn't see well enough to use his gun, not with Ruth so near Stillman. He had to separate her from Stillman, somehow.

He had to go in there, among the arches, in the dark, and find him.

Replacing the gag, Stillman said to Ruth in almost a whisper, "I guess our friend doesn't think as much of you as we both thought. I'll have to go out there to get him. Don't worry, though," he added, chucking her beneath the chin after the gag was in place, "you and I will get together later."

The two men moved cautiously in the dark, one with a knife in his hand, the other with a holstered gun. Both men were moving by instinct, and the man with the sharper instinct would come out alive.

Neither man spoke; they just continued to move from pillar to pillar. Occasionally there would be the scrape of a heel drawing one man's attention, but before he could move the other man would be gone.

A third man moved through the darkness, and his presence would have a profound effect on the outcome of this . . .fencing match.

Clint was circling to his right when suddenly he sensed that there was more than one presence ahead of him. The only thing was—he felt sure that the man ahead of him wasn't aware of him, but he was aware of the other person. Quickly Clint figured that Ruth was tied up somewhere, so she wasn't the third presence in the dark.

Whoever it was was in trouble.

●   ●   ●

Suddenly, the darkened arena beneath the bridge was bathed in streaks of moonlight as the moon escaped through a hole in the clouds.

Three men stood transfixed and the man in the center—Stillman—made a serious mistake in his haste—a mistake no professional should have made.

"Adams!" Stillman shouted triumphantly, but the man he lunged at with his knife was not Clint Adams. It was the bogus Pinkerton man, Dick Hoyt.

Clint saw the blade penetrate Hoyt's clothing and bite into his side, drawing blood.

"Stillman!" Clint called.

Stillman had withdrawn the blade and was about to thrust with it again when he turned in the direction of Clint Adams's voice.

"Adams?" he said, puzzled.

"Put the knife down, Stillman," Clint ordered. "It's all over."

He could see by the expression on Stillman's face that the man had the solution to this situation all figured out, just waiting for the time to arrive.

"Oh, no, Adams," Stillman said. "There's only one way it's all over for men like you and me."

He began to advance on Clint, knife held straight out ahead of him. He wanted Clint to kill him, and the Gunsmith knew that he couldn't allow a professional killer like Stillman to get within arm's distance with a knife.

"Stillman, don't do this," Clint said, dropping his hand to his gun.

"What you mean is don't make you do this, huh?" Stillman said, laughing. "Come on, Adams," Stillman said, "draw! Isn't that what they say where you come from? Show me that famous Gunsmith move."

Clint was trying to come up with a solution other than gunning him when suddenly there was a shot, an incredibly loud, echoing shot and Stillman looked as if someone had punched him in the back. His mouth opened and a look of total shock came over his face. His knife fell from nerveless fingers, blood poured from his mouth, and he fell on his face.

Behind him Dick Hoyt stood, one hand pressed to the wound in his side, the other hand holding a gun. In the center of Stillman's back was a hole; slowly a red stain widened around it.

Hoyt walked up to the body, faced Clint across it, and said, "Well, I guess that bounty's collected."

Clint closed his fist and drove it into Hoyt's face. The man squawked, dropped his gun, staggered back a few steps, and then fell onto his backside, staring up at Clint.

"What the hell—"

"Hoyt, you'd better pick yourself up and get the hell out of here."

"What's wrong with you?" Hoyt asked, staggering to his feet. His lips were cut and blood ran down to his chin and dripped off.

"You're a coward," Clint said.

"I saved your life."

"You shot him in the back!" Clint shouted, angrier than he'd been in a long time. "Nobody deserves to be shot from behind, Hoyt, especially by a coward."

"Adams—"

"You'd better move, Hoyt," Clint said, trying to control his rage, "while you can still walk."

"The bounty—"

"The bounty's yours, but make damn sure I don't see you collecting it."

Hoyt frowned at Clint, but something he saw in the

Gunsmith's eyes made him pick up his gun, holster it, press his left hand to his side and move off. He glanced back at the Gunsmith a couple of times, then moved away at an increasingly rapid pace.

Clint stared down at Stillman, shot from behind like Hickok—the only thing the two men had in common. He drove all thoughts of Hickok from his mind and went to find Ruth McDonald.

THIRTY-FOUR

It was Fletcher himself who showed up at his hotel the day Clint was leaving New York. Clint had been expecting someone from the police department, but not the captain himself.

The Countess, Angelina Margarita de la Fortuna—who Clint would always think of as Angela Fortune—had already left New York. He hadn't seen her since the day Stillman was killed, but he had a strong feeling he'd be seeing her again.

He had not seen Ruth either since that day. She had been too shaken by what had happened and had simply said good-bye to him that night. He couldn't blame her for that. She had been through a lot, and he hadn't treated her very well.

The police had collected Stillman's body from beneath the bridge, thereby closing the murder cases of both J.T. Archer and Henry, the tailor.

Clint had paid a last visit to the *Herald* building to inform the editor of the Gunsmith books that he would take legal action if he ever saw another one. Upon arriving, he found a new man in the editorial seat—Bennett had fired the other one all the way from Europe—and the new man had seen it the Gunsmith's way.

Now, Fletcher was waiting in the lobby when Clint came down with his bag, only two days after the incident beneath the bridge.

"On your way, I see," Fletcher said as Clint approached the desk to settle his bill.

"I've had enough of your big city, Captain."

"Can't say I blame you for that."

"What brings you here?"

"I just thought I'd stop by to see if you were leaving today."

"You mean make sure I was leaving."

"Yeah, I guess you could say that. I'm looking forward to getting things calmed down, the way they were before you arrived."

"You can hardly blame me for that," Clint said, but he wasn't truly concerned. "What about Boss Kelly?"

"What about him?"

Clint stared at Fletcher and then slowly shook his head.

"Look, Adams," Fletcher said, "I can't tie Boss Kelly to Stillman. There's no way."

"Sure," Clint said, "Hoyt saw to that. He killed Stillman, the only possible link to Kelly."

Clint's only consolation here was that Stillman was the one who had actually killed J.T. He felt that he had been hired by Boss Kelly, but Fletcher was right. There was just no way to prove it.

Hopefully, Boss Kelly would eventually get what was coming to him.

"Hoyt," Fletcher said. "Imagine a Pinkerton turning bounty hunter?"

"Did he collect?"

"He collected, and then he left town like his ass was on fire."

"Which is just what I'm about to do, Captain," Clint said, turning away from the desk and picking up his borrowed suitcase.

"Can I—uh—give you a ride to the station?" Fletcher asked, as if the offer pained him.

Surprised, Clint hesitated, then said, "I'd appreciate that, Captain. Those horse-carts are filthy and, to tell you the truth, I appreciate your offer."

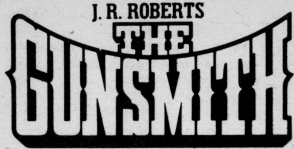

J. R. ROBERTS
THE GUNSMITH

SERIES

Prices may be slightly higher in Canada.

Available at your local bookstore or return this form to:

CHARTER BOOKS
Book Mailing Service
P.O. Box 690, Rockville Centre, NY 11571

Please send me the titles checked above. I enclose _____. Include 75¢ for postage and handling if one book is ordered; 25¢ per book for two or more not to exceed $1.75. California, Illinois, New York and Tennessee residents please add sales tax.

NAME_____

ADDRESS_____

CITY_____STATE/ZIP_____

(allow six weeks for delivery.)   **A1/a**